THE MURDER
TRAP

THE AUDREY MURDERS

LEONIE MATEER

For lovers of murder & mayhem

CHAPTER 1

Checking her cell phone, Audrey confirmed what she already knew. It was three thirty. The cottage was in complete darkness. A power cut meant no running water, no hot cup of tea, no heat, no middle of the night TV movie and her laptop computer was low on battery. She turned on the computer to drain the last few breaths of power with Leonard Cohen's "I'm your Man" and looked out the window into the moonlight. A fishing boat was lit like the fourth of July - its bright colored lights shimmered across the dark waters of the bay. The last couple of days had been stormy, rainy and cold. She presumed the weather had enticed the boats to take shelter inside the bay.

Audrey's chosen lifestyle of living in rural isolation came with its disadvantages. Fallen trees, hillside slips and storm damage caused regular power outages. She hoped her guests were sleeping through the inconvenience.

The sound of whirring broke the dark silence as electrical devices stirred into life. Audrey was too stimulated to sleep. She made a cup of coffee and checked her email. There it was. He had replied.

CHAPTER 2

G rant Pratt's life had taken a downward spiral – financially, emotionally and physically. He had a choice to make – to install insulation or take a trip up north. The winter had been cruel to his arthritis but it was almost spring, with a promise of warmer days. He couldn't say the same for his love life.

Her email was encouraging - a possibility even of solving his problematic lifestyle. She owned a rural resort in the far north. He was invited for a visit – a champagne lunch on the front lawn. It sounded rather extravagant and enticing. They had been communicating for a couple of weeks. He had found her on a dating site.

Grant's appearance was tall, lanky and rugged. His personality was in stark contrast. The man was weak and small-minded. He preyed off others, scrounging for unwanted belongings and handouts. Today would be no exception. He rode his timeworn bicycle to the local pub and waited for Bob to take his usual seat by the bar - a lunchtime ritual for the locals who came from neighboring farms for the famous fish chowder special.

"Could you do me a favor mate?" Grant asked as he accepted the offer of a beer from his good friend.

"What's that?" Bob guzzled his beer thirstily wiping the froth with the back of his hand.

"I need to borrow a car for a trip up north."

"Watcha got up north that's so important?"

"Found myself a lady – a good one. She lives up in Hihi."

"What would a lady want with you?" Bob said with half-hearted humor. "Does she know what you look like?"

"Yep. Sent her a picture. She owns a fancy cabin resort. I'll be back tomorrow night. Just a trip up and down."

"All that way for a visit? She hasn't invited you to stay then?"

"Would you mind if she did? Do you need your car for the next couple of days?"

"Nope, can use my truck. My wife has her own car. Stop by my place and I'll get you the keys. But look after her, eh? She's got a lot of miles on her but still runs pretty good."

When Grant picked up the old jeep he dropped off a bag of spuds from his garden. He hoped the jeep was full of petrol. He figured it would cost about three hundred in gas for the round trip. Grant had one hundred and twenty dollars. Maybe he could make it a one-way trip and Audrey would invite him to stay. He could see himself helping the nice looking blonde run her country resort. He certainly wouldn't miss his run-down cabin in the rural outskirts of Thames. He turned on the key and watched as the petrol indicator read almost empty. Bloody Hell! He wished he hadn't parted with the spuds. Bloody cheap shit! He would need to borrow a couple of hundred dollars now to make the trip. He returned to the pub hopeful.

CHAPTER 3

Bored. Audrey was bored. When she was bored she had two options; find a new project or a new romance. The latter took less effort and, if it didn't work out, she could combine the two. Winter was always slow for business. Apart from a few fishermen and a long-term guest, her cabins were mostly vacant. She had a couple of months before the summer holiday traffic – just enough time for a romantic interlude.

Her online search had resulted in two possibilities and one was coming up this weekend. He was a good-looking man. She liked her men tall and lean and Grant fit the profile perfectly. She guessed he was retired, as he never mentioned his work. They shared the same lifestyle interests – living rural and isolated. He grew his own vegetables, cut firewood for his neighbors and sounded like a kind, giving man. She hadn't suggested he stay overnight. She would wait until they met to confirm any mutual chemistry. Her last romantic affair was with a woman, causing a realization she was bi. She had invited the man to lunch on the lawn. She liked the sound of it. Reminded her of the English gentry from British movies and television sagas, which she watched with a morbid fascination.

Audrey was looking wonderful. At least she thought so after years of no sugar and no dairy. Age had smiled on Audrey lately, giving her a new vibrancy and energy only a good diet and lots of champagne could explain. Her hair, freshly died a pretty tobacco blonde and cut in a long bob, accented her green eyes and long lashes. Clothes that used to cause her such a dilemma now seemed easy to find and easy to wear. Her choice for her afternoon date was soft, feminine and sexually enticing.

The day was perfect. Blue skies with a wisp of cloud replaced the gray days of the past with a sparkle equaling her own vivacity. A new umbrella shaded the picnic table set for expectations only the naïve could dream. Perfection and timeliness were two attributes Audrey owned and respected in others. Anything less caused irretrievable damage.

She poured a glass of chilled champagne and looked at the time. If she didn't hear his car in the next few minutes he would be late. Her fears were unfounded. She watched as an old, dusty Jeep drove up her driveway and parked next to her Rav4. Her heart missed a beat as she watched a wonderful specimen of a man straighten slowly to a standing position holding a bunch of wild white lilies – her favorite.

CHAPTER 4

I mpressive! Grant liked what he saw as he passed the blue waters of Doubtless Bay and headed up the gravel road towards his future. The long narrow driveway precariously bordered by tall bent pine trees sent a small shiver down his spine. A premonition? A warning? He wondered. He didn't have a penny to his name and this might be his last chance of finding love and, much more importantly, eternal financial security.

There she was. Waving and smiling. Too good for him. Shit! She had everything. He could offer nothing. He picked up the lilies he had found growing on the side of the road, took a deep breath, checked his reflection in the rear vision mirror and stepped out to face his destiny.

Grant, having led a relatively mundane life, realized over lunch, Audrey had never lived an ordinary day in her life. Her exuberant nature and love of everything that looked, tasted or smelled pleasurable was an obvious peek into a lifetime of plenty. They couldn't be more dissimilar. He knew if she discovered his ordinariness she would simply bid him farewell and he wasn't planning on going anywhere. His livelihood depended on charming her enough to be asked to stay.

"I would love a tour." Grant returned his empty glass to the table. "How long have you owned this wonderful resort? I must say you have done a wonderful job here."

Audrey was proud of her business. It had taken every penny she owned and could borrow to build the self-contained cabins on the fourteen-acre property overlooking Doubtless Bay. Two private beaches and romantic bush walkways meandered along the ridges and down to the water's edge, providing her guests with rural pleasures they couldn't experience in the cities.

"It has been a few years now." Audrey began to clear the table. "There was only one cabin when I first moved here. Now there are six. It is the quiet time now but it gets really busy in the summer season."

"Here, let me help you," he offered collecting the empty champagne bottle and glasses. "I bet the fishing is great here."

"It is. The beach below Rocky Ridge is well known as a local fishing spot. If you like we could take a walk down there. It is such a lovely afternoon."

He followed her into her cottage and placed the glasses on the bench while she rinsed off their dishes and left them in the sink.

"Let's go," she said grabbing a big yellow sunhat and changing into a pair of pink and yellow sneakers. "If we are lucky we may be able to walk along the shore to the next beach. It is only accessible from the shore when the tide is out."

Grant hoped the walk would give him time to charm his way into her heart. She was a lovely little thing. All bounce and boobs. He wondered why she lived alone.

As they passed the cabins he asked, "are all the cabins occupied?"

"No." she replied cautiously.

CHAPTER 5

S he was looking out the cabin window as they walked towards Rocky Beach. Poppy was curious. She had taken a long-term rental of the Kiwi Cabin to write her book. The quiet seclusion and rural setting provided a perfect location for creative writing.

Poppy was writing about murder. She had researched the spree of murders that had taken place in the far north. Bodies had even washed up on the shores of Doubtless Bay. The cases had fascinated her. Why so many murders in such an isolated place? Later today she had an appointment with the local detective, Inspector Bromley. He had been the lead detective on a number of the cases.

The resort owner, Audrey Wetherby, had given her a great winter rate on the cabin. Such a strange woman - all smiles and pleasantness. But Poppy didn't trust the woman. She watched as they disappeared down the road to the beach. The man was tall and gangly. Nice looking but she could tell he didn't come from the same class as Audrey. His shoes were worn and his jeans were cheap and ill fitting. She wondered if he was a friend or someone looking to stay at the resort.

This was her first day in the cabin and she had spent the morning unpacking and setting up a workstation on the dining table. The cabin was completely self-sufficient - a small kitchen, big screen TV, comfy sofa and queen-size bed. The tiled bathroom provided both a bath and a shower. It was exactly what she needed for her six week stay. Next Thursday was the first day of spring and the weather should be getting warmer.

Feeling a little restless, Poppy decided to take a walk down to the resort's private beaches. Of course no-one could legally own a beach in New Zealand, but the resort apparently owned up to the high tide level meaning public access was only possible during low tide. The resort had two beaches: Rocky Beach and Honeymoon Beach. Rocky Beach was accessible by a private gravel road. The resort only allowed access by foot as the road was steep and the turning area at the shore was difficult to maneuver. Honeymoon Beach was accessible by a track down the ridge in front of the office and owner's cottage. It was a challenging climb by rope down a hundred clay steps cut from the steep bank. Both tracks were out of sight from the shore and fishermen who walked the shoreline to access the beaches were unaware of the resort accesses.

Poppy had done her research. The resort had been the center of many of the murder locations. Guests' bodies had been found washed up on the beaches below and Audrey Wetherby's resort was a constant thread throughout the investigations. Audrey, however, had never been a suspect in any of the crimes. Poppy felt differently.

As Poppy headed down Rocky Ridge Road she saw Audrey and the tall man approaching. "Beautiful day," she said, as they passed on the steep incline.

"Yes, it is lovely to see the sun again."

She turned and watched the pair disappear around the bend.

CHAPTER 6

Audrey had decided to let her date stay the night. It was late when they finished dinner and she didn't have the heart to make him take the seven-hour drive back to Thames. Instead she gave him the key to the Morepork Cabin and bade him goodnight.

The night had not gone well. Their walk down to the beach had been enjoyable and the conversation pleasant. All that changed when they returned to her cottage and drank their second bottle of wine. He had become rather crude and obnoxious – a reminder why she had chosen not to remarry.

She looked up as the man entered her office.

"Lovely night we had."

Audrey wondered why men were so ignorant when it came to reading a woman's mind.

"Lovely" she lied.

"So what is on the schedule for today?" The man looked so eager and far too hopeful.

"I have to get back to work. Have a busy day ahead of me." Audrey had a feeling the man was not planning on leaving any time soon. "It looks as though we are in for another sunny day. You should have a nice trip back."

"I was hoping to stay another night or two. Get to know each other."

"I am so sorry, but I am fully booked tonight. I have a fishing group arriving any time now and have to get the cabins ready." *It's a lie* "But it has been a pleasure meeting you. I wish you all the best." *Just leave.*

Audrey watched as the tall, lean man stood defiantly in her office.

"I could always share your bed."

Fuck, I guess I have to spell it out. "I don't think so, but", *Oh shit, I have forgotten his name.* "I really wish you all the best on your search for love."

He got mad. "Well that is that then. You know it cost me a fortune to drive up here. You really are a bit of a tease. Aren't you? Getting me to come all the way up here on a promise and then just chuck me out!"

She had heard it all before. Men. She didn't know why she bothered. It was the thought of closeness, tenderness, gentleness, kindness, even. Instead, now she just wanted to kill them.

"I'm sorry you feel that way."

"Excuse me." Her pretty female guest entered the office. "I was just heading into the village and wanted to know if you could recommend a good stationers? I need to pick up an ink cartridge for my printer."

Audrey was pleased for the interruption. "It all depends on what cartridge you need. I have to go into Waipapa or Kaitaia for my cartridges. The local stationery store in Mangonui only has a limited selection. You might want to call them first. "Here." Audrey handed the woman a card from the store.

"You are most kind. Thank you."

"Well, I guess I'll be off then," the man said.

"Have a safe journey." Audrey dismissed him and asked the woman "How long do you think you will be staying? You mentioned a few weeks?"

"I don't know for sure. Can I let you know in a day or two?" she replied.

Audrey was curious. "You have friends or family nearby?"

"No, just here to get some work done." The woman replied noncommittally.

"What sort of work do you do? If you don't mind me asking?"

"No, not at all. I am starting a new online travel magazine. Working my way from the top of the country to the bottom."

"That is wonderful. I hope you say nice things about Tiromoana." Audrey smiled. "If you need to know anything about the local restaurants and sights, let me know," she offered.

"Will do. Mostly it is just gathering loads of information and getting it uploaded. But thanks."

Audrey watched as the woman followed the man down the path towards their parked cars. What a nice woman. She didn't give the man another thought.

CHAPTER 7

Detective Inspector Bromley was still reeling at his recent promotion. The sheer number of solved murders in his territory had put him on the fast track for promotions. Now he had to live up to his Super's expectations.

He smelled her before he saw her - a sweet fragrance, sexy, alluring. Her voice was as sultry as her essence. "I have an appointment with Detective Inspector Bromley?" he heard from the front office.

He waited for Constable Williams to escort her into his office and he wasn't disappointed. Bromley had never been unfaithful to his wife. Never. Not in all the years they had been together. This woman, however, simply took his breath away. She was stunning!

"Poppy Perkins," the woman held out her hand in anticipation of a professional greeting.

"Detective Inspector Bromley," he replied. "What can I do for you?" *Warm hands. Soft hands.*

"I am a writer of true crime books, and have been told, you

are the person I need to talk to regarding the excessive number of murders in your community over the past few years."

Her eyes were sky blue and serious. "Yes, thank goodness things have quieted down. You do realize that the murders were not related. Different crimes, different perpetrators."

"I have my suspicions about that," she pulled out a notebook from her bag. "Most of the murders took place in or near Hihi. Didn't you find it strange that they took place in one remote location but yet multiple perpetrators were found guilty? You never suspected a local Hihi resident of any of the crimes?"

Bromley felt a little intimidated. She was so serious, almost angry. "As I have explained, the crimes were not related."

"Are you sure? Can you honestly tell me it has never entered your mind that you may have a serial killer living in your community?"

Bromley laughed. "You have been watching too much television. Believe me. If we had a serial killer among us, I would know."

"I wouldn't be too sure of that," Poppy Perkins closed her notebook without writing a single word. Maybe you won't find this so amusing when I prove you wrong."

Bromley felt a little ashamed "I'm sorry I couldn't be more help. Are there any particular cases you are featuring in your book?"

"Well, yes. The case involving the young teen girl whose body was found in Doubtless Bay. It was reported she was a prostitute. Her killer was staying at Tiromoana Cabins. He supposedly committed suicide. Which seemed a little too convenient." She stood to leave. "I am also researching the death of Constable Higgins whose body also ended up in Doubtless Bay. I have read the court files and there are a lot of questions left unanswered."

"Well, if I can be of further help, please let me know." The detective shook her outstretched hand once again.

She smiled at him. He felt her gaze and looked away hoping she hadn't seen the effect she had on him. "Thank you, I will," she said. "By the way, I would prefer no-one knows why I am here. Can we keep this between us?"

Bromley was amused by her cloak and dagger approach "Absolutely, no problem. My lips are sealed." He walked her out to the front office and watched her leave in a little red Mazda MX-5 convertible.

Suddenly Bromley had an ominous feeling of foreboding. Dragging up the old case involving his daughter's friend would not be welcomed. His daughter had been out with her that fateful night. The night the girl had been taken from the street corner in Taipa and murdered. No-one knew his daughter had been involved. And no-one would. He had made sure of that.

He wished he had asked Ms. Poppy Perkins where she was staying.

CHAPTER 8

Steve Sutton was a man's man. Having spent most of his sixty-three years mining and farming he had made himself a small fortune. All he needed now was a good woman to clean, cook and take care of his sexual needs. This was his second attempt at an Asian mail-order bride. It was back in the nineties when he brought his first one over. She was a little thing. Timid. It worked fine for the first few months then she started to get a little antsy. He decided a trip back to visit her family in the Philippines might cheer her up. It was a disaster. He knew her family was poor but he never imagined such poverty. When he realized he was expected to support her whole family once they were married, he left her there. This time it would be different.

His new soon-to-be bride was from China and from a good family. She was coming over to New Zealand to study and was looking for a New Zealand man to marry. He presumed it was so she could gain permanent residency. She spoke English, which was a good thing. OK, so she was only twenty-two and he was a little older. But she said she never minded his age. She was arriving at Auckland airport first thing tomorrow morning.

He looked around his house and decided the mess could stay where it was. The girl could clean it up. Would give her something to do.

Steve checked his appearance in the full-length mirror. He was not what one would call a good-looking man. His hair was thinning, his stomach protruding and his stature was short. His mates called him "Stumpy." He had never been successful with the ladies. Prostitutes were legal and plentiful, and he had certainly enjoyed their expertise over the years. He had purchased his hundred-acre block of land on the Hihi Peninsula a few months ago and the nearest brothel was at least two hours away. He was getting too old for prostitutes anyway.

Steve's nearest neighbor was Tiromoana Cabin Resort. He had seen the blonde owner coming and going in her old Rav4. He nearly hit her on the narrow, winding gravel road. She swerved and waved simultaneously avoiding him by inches and leaving a cloud of dust in her wake. Bloody woman! He figured she was one of the high achievers, running a business all on her own. He was looking forward to bringing his more sedate and docile wife-to-be home tomorrow.

He hoped she would know how to cook good old roast dinners and mashed spuds. He would have none of that fancy Asian food. They would stop off at the supermarket in Kerikeri on the way back from the airport so she could pick up some groceries. As for her studies, he hoped she wouldn't bother. After all, her main duties would be running the home and taking care of him. He poured himself a stiff scotch, turned on the news and looked across the bay at the setting sun.

CHAPTER 9

Detective Inspector Bromley couldn't get the woman out of his mind. Poppy Perkins. She looked like a Poppy. He decided to take a drive up to Hihi. There were only a couple of places she could stay there - the motor camp motels or Tiromoana. It had been a while since he had driven up Peninsula Road. In fact it had been quite a few months. His Uncle used to own the property next door to Audrey's place. It was sold to a retired farmer from the Waikato.

As he headed down Mangonui's waterfront, he saw her red convertible parked outside the corner restaurant. He pulled in beside it and approached her sitting alone at an outside table. "Ms. Perkins, what a surprise."

"Morning Detective. Would you like to join me for a cup of coffee? Or would that get the local tongues a-wagging?" she joked.

Bromley felt himself blush. Damn, that woman! "I am a happily married man with three girls and a clear conscience," he replied and immediately regretted his obvious over exposure.

"So that is a yes?" she smiled.

Bromley went inside and ordered a coffee and a couple of lemon tarts and returned to the woman outside. "I hope you have a sweet tooth?"

"I do." Poppy looked very serious. "Tell me Detective, your daughter was friends with the girl found in the bay. Did she know her friend was prostituting herself?"

"No. She had no idea. They went to a movie that night and my daughter returned home and the girl stayed behind saying she was meeting her boyfriend. It took my daughter quite some time to recover from the loss of her friend."

"But she is fine now? I don't suppose I could talk to her?"

"I would prefer you didn't. Dragging it all up again would only undo all the good the therapist has done."

"So she was seeing a therapist?"

"For a few months afterwards."

The detective quickly changed the subject. "So, tell me. Where are you staying while you are writing this book of yours?"

"Oh, didn't I say? I am staying at Audrey's place, Tiromoana."

"Isn't that a bit risky considering you are wanting to keep your investigation confidential?"

"No, Audrey thinks I am setting up a new travel website." She laughed. "I guess I had better start writing some reviews. What do you think of your coffee and lemon tart?"

"Excellent. Five stars!" he realized he was enjoying himself. "I don't suppose you know anyone in town?"

"Only you. Oh, and Audrey, of course."

"I would be happy to take you around to the locations where the bodies were found. I am taking my boat out tomorrow if you would like to do a little research." *Shit what am I doing?*

"That would be fantastic! What time?"

"Give me your phone number and I'll call you. But plan about three o'clock."

Poppy reached over and picked up the detective's cell phone from the table and entered her number. Bromley was excited and surprised by such a personal reaction to his request.

"Tomorrow then." Poppy said as she pushed her empty plate aside and picked up her canvas bag and left the detective sitting at the table suddenly feeling exposed to the curious glances of his neighbors and friends at adjoining tables. *Damn! This will take about thirty seconds to get back to Mary. What was I thinking!* The detective knew what he was thinking, and it wasn't about the crimes she was interested in. He was thinking about spending time with Poppy Perkins on his boat tomorrow afternoon.

CHAPTER 10

Grant Pratt wasn't going anywhere. Fuck Audrey Wetherby! Brings me all the way up here and throws me out. Stuck up bitch! He had spent the night sleeping in his friend's jeep down an old track off Peninsula Road, by the waterfront. He figured the property belonged to Audrey. There was a big "Private Property" sign on the corner where he turned off. Well fuck her!

The early spring night had been cold and the jeep was drafty and smelled of cow dung. He checked his cash supply. It wasn't good. He had a choice - spend the last few dollars on gas or buy breakfast. He decided on breakfast. He had enough gas to drive the ten minutes to the Mangonui pub.

As he drove down the main road he spotted the woman who had interrupted him and Audrey in the office at Tiromoana. She was driving a red convertible. She certainly has a buck or two. He pulled into the pub and took a seat at the bar. He figured most of the patrons were locals, a noisy, happy lot. Mangonui was pretty much a retirement village and, looking at his drinking companions, he guessed they were sure enjoying their golden years. He ordered a feed of bacon, sausages, eggs and chips and downed a couple of beers while he waited.

"Nice day. Going fishing?" a guy in an unseasonably sleeveless t-shirt and shorts asked.

"Hadn't planned on it. Just driving through."

"Where're you from?"

"Thames. Came up to visit a friend."

"How long are you staying?"

"Was planning on heading on back today."

"Well then, have a few drinks on us," the guy said as he waved the barman over. "Another drink for my friend."

Breakfast turned into lunch - a drinking lunch. By mid afternoon, Grant Pratt decided he was too drunk to drive back to Thames. He made a fateful decision and headed back to Audrey's. *The bitch can put me up for the night and loan me a few hundred dollars. She owes me that.*

CHAPTER 11

Audrey poured herself a nice cold glass of champagne. It was getting on to four o'clock. All the guests had checked in and were happily occupied with their holiday plans. She closed the office and took her champagne out to the picnic table on the front lawn. Spring was one of her favorite times. Her gardens had appreciated the wetter-than-normal winter months and now were showering blossoms in the warm breeze.

Her guest, Ms. Perkins, had stopped by for a chat. She was quite beautiful. Audrey was seriously regretting her late night chats with Grant, a horrible man. Uncouth and foul mouthed. Looks certainly don't tell all. Ms. Perkins, on the other hand was simply divine. Audrey was looking forward to getting to know her better.

She heard a car pulling into her car park and turned to see Grant's old Jeep coming to an abrupt stop. She watched as he staggered up her driveway towards her. It was too late to make a dive inside the cottage and pretend she wasn't here. *Fuck! What does he want now?*

"I'm back," the man slurred. "Miss me?"

"I thought you were on your way to Thames?"

"Changed my mind. Decided to spend a little more time here. Didn't feel right just leaving you alone like that."

"I'm so sorry, but I explained all the cabins are fully booked tonight and the guests have all checked in. Would you like me to call the Motor Camp and see if they have a motel for tonight?"

"Nope. They are full too," he lied. "I guess I will be sharing your bed after all."

"No, that is not going to happen." Audrey walked to her cottage and was about to close the door in his face when he put his foot in the door, pushed it open and followed her inside.

"Please leave." Audrey asked politely. "I am sorry you came all the way up here and it didn't work out. I think we are just not compatible." Audrey realized it was futile to try and talk her way out of it. He was obviously not going anywhere.

Sitting at the table Grant asked, "Don't suppose you have a beer?"

Audrey realized that she had a problem. A problem she was only too happy to solve, but not now. Not in broad daylight. She would have to wait until dark. Thank God it wasn't daylight saving and would be pitch black by nine o'clock. She walked into the kitchen and reached for a small bottle on the top shelf of her pantry. GHB. It always worked. She combined it with a nice long cold beer and handed it to her guest.

"Well, we may as well have a drink while I put on some dinner. Chicken soup OK with you?"

Grant looked so happy he had won the battle. He took a long gulp of beer and burped. "Chicken Soup works for me."

CHAPTER 12

Poppy knew she had to be careful. There was no doubt in her mind Audrey Wetherby was linked to every murder she was researching. Poppy knew she had the advantage. Audrey had no idea she was on to her. Poppy's laptop contained her phony new travel business complete with website, Twitter account and blogs. All her research and notes on the murders were on a memory stick, which she kept with her at all times. If Audrey became suspicious in any way and searched her cabin, Poppy's real intentions would be protected.

It was a lovely evening and having purchased a nice bottle of wine in the local Four Square shop in the village she wondered if she could entice Audrey to join her in a drink. She grabbed the bottle and a couple of glasses and made her way up the ridge to the office.

Finding the office closed, she walked next door to the cottage. As she approached the sliding glass doors, she noticed the curtains were pulled and she could hear a man's voice - loud and obnoxious. Poppy wondered if it was the same rude man she had seen with Audrey the day before. Why on earth would someone like Audrey be hanging out with such an abusive guy? Maybe he was a relative. She decided not to disturb them and made her way back to her cabin.

Poppy was looking forward to tomorrow's meeting with Detective Bromley. He was a good-looking man and she knew he was attracted to her. He blushed when she handed him his phone. She wondered if he would tell his wife he was taking her out on his boat. She doubted it. Men didn't usually share that type of information with their wives. What they don't know won't hurt them. Poppy knew she could use her charm to get what she wanted. And she wanted to know more about the murders in Doubtless Bay. The Detective was responsible for arresting the perpetrators. Poppy knew he had got it wrong. She had a personal interest in one of the cases. And she knew something the detective didn't. But she was not going to share this information with anyone. She would wait until she had proof. Proof that Audrey Wetherby was a serial killer.

CHAPTER 13

Dinnertime at the Bromley's had changed over the years. What used to be family time was now couple time. The girls had all left for college in Auckland. They had a flat in the city and would come home for holidays. Mary had not taken well to the girls leaving home. The last five years had not been kind to her. Bromley had noticed she no longer dyed her hair or attended her yoga classes. Their sex life was non- existent. He hoped grandchildren would perk her up. His oldest daughter, Lucy, was engaged to be married. Mary would have the wedding to look forward to at least.

He poured them both a glass of wine and they sat in silence eating the casserole of lamb chops and kumera. Mary was a wonderful cook. "So how was your day?" he asked.

"I picked up a couple of books from the library and ran into Barb. She said she saw you having coffee at the corner café with a young woman this morning."

Shit. There it is. "Yes, she came into the police station yesterday and I promised to get her some information concerning a friend of hers."

"Oh."

The silence was deafening. "It is police business and I cannot really talk about it," he said closing the conversation.

"I see."

Bromley knew he had crossed over the line. He had lied. To protect her? To protect his wife? To protect himself? Or all three? "By the way, I am taking the boat out tomorrow afternoon on police business. I won't be back for dinner. Could be late."

"Fine. It'll give me a chance to watch that French movie."

CHAPTER 14

The tall, lean man was out cold sprawled on her kitchen floor. She had pulled all the curtains and turned out the lights. She checked - he was still breathing, but it was very shallow. His Jeep was in the driveway. As soon as it was dark, she would need to take his car and dispose of them both.

Audrey didn't like to be unprepared. His obnoxious assumptions and threats gave her no choice. He had to go. Bloody men! Why couldn't he just have returned to where he came from? She had tried to be nice. What right did he have to demand she take responsibility for their obvious incompatibility?

She presumed he had been in a nearby pub in order to get so hammered. Seen by locals. This could be an advantage. A drunk driving accident would be easily explained.

She checked his pulse again. Still ticking. *Damn!* Audrey reached for the cushion on her leather bucket chair and held it firmly over the man's face. It didn't take long. Grant Pratt was dead.

She found the man's keys in his pocket and, checking no-one was in sight, left her dead date on the floor, headed up the path to the man's shitty old Jeep and drove it up the isolated Peninsula Road. She parked the car, off the road, out of sight and returned home on foot.

The pressure was off. She had until daybreak to dispose of the man. Audrey pulled the throw blanket off the sofa, dropped it over the body and went to bed. If there was one thing Audrey had learned over the years; 'if you want to solve a problem, sleep on it.' She set the alarm for three am and fell asleep.

Audrey awoke feeling rejuvenated, excited. The memories of the previous night came into focus. She stepped over the body and made herself a nice cup of tea and a couple of slices of multi grain toast with vegemite. Looking outside she could see the stars. It was a clear night and a half moon. Too much light to drag a body out into the open and pop it in the back of her car. She would have to disguise the body.

She grabbed a large sheep pellet sack, furniture dolly and a couple of bungee cords from the garden shed and returned to the cottage.

Grant Perkins took his place on the dolly covered in sheep feed and ceremoniously escorted out of the cottage into the back of Audrey's Rav4. Not an easy task but one Audrey had perfected over the years.

Quietly she drove up Peninsula Road and parked next to the Jeep and off-loaded her disappointing date into the driver's seat. It wasn't difficult to park the Jeep close to the cliff, put it in drive and watch it disappear into the night.

By the time she returned to the cottage and into bed it was still a few hours before dawn. She sighed a deep breath. *Bloody Men!* And fell instantly into a dreamless sleep.

CHAPTER 15

Poppy Perkins hadn't slept well. Earlier in the evening she saw the old Jeep leaving down the driveway. She recognized it as the tall man's Jeep – the man who had been arguing with Audrey the day she checked in. It must have been him she had heard in her cottage. Early in the morning she was awoken to the sound of a car leaving and returning about twenty minutes afterwards. She had looked at the time - it was four o'clock.

She guessed it might be the fishermen who checked in yesterday. Her dad was a fisherman; he too liked to be on the water before dawn.

It was going to be a nice day - blue sky and fluffy white clouds. Perfect. She would do research in the morning, take a lunch in the village and hopefully take a trip on the bay in the afternoon.

Poppy had been busy. Researching recent crimes in Hihi, Mangonui, Kaeo and Whangaroa produced an abundance of information. Bodies ravaged by wild pigs, deaths by oleander poisoning, bodies dumped in Doubtless Bay, suspicious suicide on the Hihi peninsula and there was always one person who was in the midst of the cases; Audrey Wetherby. Poppy had a personal interest in one of the cases. She would not only prove Audrey was responsible for her brother's death, but she would make sure she was locked up for life. Audrey Wetherby was a dangerous person.

Poppy looked out her cabin window and saw Audrey carrying a pile of fresh linens to one of the cabins. It was almost mid-day. Time to put her work away and head off into Mangonui for lunch and a chat with the locals.

She checked her phone; there was a text message from Detective Inspector Bromley. *Meet me at the Mangonui wharf at 3p.m.* Perfect! She would bring her camera and take pictures of the crime scenes.

CHAPTER 16

Bob Stark was getting pissed off. He had tried calling old Pratt a dozen times. He obviously had not returned from his hot date in Northland. Back in one day, my arse. He had been gone three days and he hadn't heard a peek out of him. He needed his Jeep. Pratt was a cheap shit and refused to own a cell phone. He decided to go around to his house and see if he had returned and was just not bothering to answer his phone.

The back door was always unlocked. Pratt's house was a dump. Empty beer cans, dirty dishes in the sink, open cans of food on the bench and huge piles of clothes covered the sofa and spilled onto the floor. There was no sign of Pratt. Bob found his old desktop computer in his bedroom and hoped it would provide some information about where he had gone and with whom he was visiting.

Bob was proud of his computer skills. His daughter had shown him how to use Facebook, access his banking online and even use email. He checked Pratt's in-box. There it was. He was emailing an Audrey Wetherby. She had even obliged him with driving directions to her place in Hihi. He did a search and found her phone number. She was the owner of the Tiromoana Cabins in Hihi. He guessed old Pratt had checked himself in and had not bothered to call him. Guess he got lucky!

When Bob returned home he called the number and spoke to Ms. Wetherby. "Yes, hello there. I was wondering if I could have a word to my friend, Grant Pratt."

"Oh. I am sorry but Grant Pratt checked out a couple of days ago.

"I understand he was coming up to meet you. I *am* speaking to Audrey Wetherby?"

"Yes, this is she. He stayed in our Morepork Cabin on Saturday night and checked out the following morning. I presumed he was heading home. Are you sure he hasn't returned?"

"Nope. No sign of him here. He has my old Jeep and I was expecting him back a couple of days ago. If you should see him can you ask him to call Bob Stark?"

"Will do. I'm sorry I can't be of more help to you."

Fuck! Bob was getting really annoyed with Pratt now. He never should have agreed to loan him his Jeep. He guessed Pratt had stopped off on his way back to Thames on a pub-crawl, no doubt. He knew he was a heavy drinker. Where he got the money to keep himself constantly intoxicated, he had no idea. Always pleading poverty was Pratt.

He would give him another couple of days and then see if he could track him down. By the sounds of Ms. Wetherby, Pratt had obviously not won any points with her. She sounded way too hoity-toity for old Pratt.

CHAPTER 17

H e watched her walking down the jetty. Stunning. Her hair blowing loose in the wind. She had a body to die for. Her tight jeans, white cashmere sweater and pale blue scarf were pure femininity. If he didn't know better he would say he was in love.

"What an absolutely perfect day." She took his hand as he helped her aboard. "Thank you so much for doing this for me. It will really help me with my research knowing exactly where the bodies were found. I hope I don't get you into trouble?"

"It will be our little secret" *Damn, I am flirting with her.* "Would you like a drink? Wine? Beer?"

"A wine would be wonderful. Thank you," She saw him blush when their hands touched as he passed her a glass of Dashwood Sauvignon Blanc. "So where are we heading first?"

"I don't know if you remember, but a couple of years ago there was a cocaine smuggling case and the perpetrators were staying at Audrey's cabins. It was discovered to be part of a nationwide brothel distribution racket. The body of one of the

Mexican drug dealers was found washed up over there." He pointed to a rocky cove near Audrey's beach.

A few minutes later, he pointed to another rocky inlet "That's where they found my friend, Detective Hutton. He had fallen off the rock while fishing, hit his head and drowned. Awful. He was a good guy."

"Isn't that Audrey's Rocky Beach? There is a road leading down to the beach from Tiromoana."

"Yes, he was off duty at the time and doing some of his own surveillance. He suspected Audrey had something to do with the death of her parents."

"And you have never suspected Audrey of any of these murders?"

"Of course we looked at her, but eventually we caught the perpetrators responsible for each crime. It was pure coincidence that many of the crimes took place at or near her residence or business."

"And the murders at Whangaroa. You did know she owned the Three Suites where the bones were found?"

"Awful. The poor guy was eaten by wild pigs. Audrey's properties just happen to be in remote locations. There are not many accommodation options up here in the far north just pubs and motels and a couple of motor camps. Her places offer a little more privacy which tends to attract people with crime on their minds."

"I just don't get it." Poppy continued to snap photos of the craggy cliffs and rocky coves. "You have never found her DNA on any of the bodies?"

"There was no need to test for her DNA. She was never a suspect of any of the crimes. She was not even a real person of interest. Audrey is harmless. She has an excellent reputation in

Northland. You just have to check out her website to see how much her guests enjoyed their stay at her establishments."

"I understand the man who murdered your daughter's friend committed suicide and so did his sister. Rather coincidental, wouldn't you say?" Poppy passed over her empty glass for a refill.

"No there was no doubt that we got the right guy for the crime. He had her personal belongings in his car and photos of the girl on his camera. He was guilty all right. He knew it would only be a matter of time before he was arrested. He chose the easy way out."

Bromley was on cloud nine. He was on his third glass of wine as he turned off the motor and let the boat drift in the quietness of the bay. Poppy leaned back on the bench seat and squinted at the late afternoon sun. A white glare covered the ocean in the distance. It was getting a little chilly. The spring weather was changeable and Poppy detected a dark cloud beginning to form.

"Maybe we should be getting back. It looks we might be getting a light shower soon."

"Yes, you are right. "He started the engine disappointed his time with her was coming to an end. When would he see her again? How could he see her again? It was a small village and gossip was rampant. He must be careful. "Please let me know if I can help you with your research. I have all the files of the cases you are researching in my office."

Poppy's face lit up with sheer pleasure. "That would be fantastic! Thank you."

As they made their way back to the dock at Mangonui they passed Tiromoana up on the hill, in the distance. She could see Audrey's cottage and office. The cabins were out of view from the bay. The waves were beginning to churn and slop as the weather worsened.

Tiromoana looked sinister in the darkening sky. The tide was in and waves were crashing dangerously against the rocks on her shoreline. Poppy felt a shiver going up her spine. Something was going on at Tiromoana. Something new. She must get back.

CHAPTER 18

A udrey watched the skies getting darker. She closed the umbrellas on the picnic tables and stacked the outside chairs in readiness for a spring shower. The wind was getting stronger, causing dead branches from the gum trees to fall on the lawns. She had heard that large falling branches from gum trees often cause death. Next time she is stupid enough to invite a strange man over for tea she would make sure she sat him under the gum tree so she didn't have to deal with him afterwards.

Grant, she guessed was still sitting in his Jeep down the rugged, steep cliff further up the peninsula. No-one was even living up there. Most of the residents only inhabited their houses during the summer months. By then, the body should be pretty much decomposed.

Unfortunately, the whole peninsula was a protected kiwi bird zone and trappers covered the area on quad bikes and on foot, setting stoat and possum traps. They would be able to smell Mr. Pratt even if they couldn't see him in the dense bush. She was pleased she had remembered to stock his Jeep with plenty of booze. Maybe she should go back and set fire to it. But it was also a no-fire zone. She had never used a fire to hide a body before. She would need to think about that.

She saw Poppy Perkins coming up the driveway as she headed back inside the cottage. A few minutes later Poppy appeared at her front door.

"I hope I am not disturbing you, but I was wondering if you would like to join me for a glass of wine and a hot tub. It is getting chilly and I thought it would be nice to warm up a bit. And I would really like some company. It gets pretty lonely around here doesn't it?"

"Yes it does. I'll meet you at your cabin in a few minutes." Audrey was flattered by this beautiful woman's invitation. "I will just get changed."

"Great. I'll see you soon." Poppy headed off across the ridge.

Audrey threw on her swimsuit and grabbed a towel and a couple of bottles of Oyster Bay and headed off in the direction of her new best friend.

CHAPTER 19

Steve Sutton looked at the shy little girl sitting in his passenger seat, "So how do I pronounce your name?" he asked.

"Mei Wong," she whispered.

"I will call you May. Soon you will be May Sutton." He grabbed her pale, small hand and gave it a big squeeze. She pulled away.

"You will like Hihi. We live on top of a cliff, overlooking Doubtless Bay. Beautiful place, one- hundred acres of bush and rolling green hills. I have a boat, quad bikes, tractor and a ride-on mower. I don't suppose you know how to drive? You could mow the lawns."

Mei shook her head. "No, I don't drive."

"Never mind. I can teach you. Do you like to swim?"

Mei shook her head.

"You will have to learn to swim and fish. Maybe we will take out the boat tomorrow. Would you like that?"

The girl nodded politely.

"You are not much of a talker, are you?" he chuckled. Steve

was pleased with his new bride-to-be. She was prettier than she looked on the dating site. She also looked a lot younger. He doubted she was twenty-two she looked more like eighteen. He was old enough to be her grandfather. He wondered why such a young girl would even consider marrying a man as old as he.

The trip from Auckland was long and tedious. The conversation was awkward and sporadic. Steve was pleased when he pulled up to his house on the cliff. It was about fifteen years old. A beautiful, modern, architecturally-designed home with floor to ceiling windows and surrounded by covered decks exposing panoramic views across the bay.

Mei followed the man inside after removing her shoes and carefully placing them on the doormat inside the door.

The house was impressive. It was a large house with four bedrooms, all with en-suite bathrooms, an office, guest quarters and open plan lounge, kitchen dining with an expansive open fireplace in the center. Steve looked for a sign of admiration on Mei's face but saw only fear.

"You don't like the house?" he asked, amazed.

"Yes, it's very nice, but very big. Lots of work to keep clean."

"Would you like to take a drive around the grounds, see the beach?"

Mei nodded.

Steve helped Mei onto the back of his quad bike and set off to tour his hundred acres through meandering tracks into the bush and down to his three private beaches.

"You have neighbors?" Mei asked.

"Just one. Audrey Wetherby. She owns the Tiromoana Cabin Resort. You would have seen the sign just before we entered my driveway. I haven't met the lady yet. I hear she is rather reclusive, but friendly.

"Where is the school for my studies?" Mei asked.

"Oh, we'll talk about that later. You have enough to keep you busy in the meantime."

"Your family? Where is your family?"

"Don't have any family." The man replied.

As they returned to the house Mei asked the man to "Please remove your shoes."

He scoffed, "Not likely."

CHAPTER 20

Poppy watched Audrey as she reached across the hot tub for her glass. "Thanks for joining me. It is really nice to have some company," she said.

"Yes, even though the cabins are often fully booked, and the place is buzzing with activity, it can still be lonely if you are on your own. Personally, I like my alone time."

"Was that your boyfriend I saw you with the other day? The man who drives the Jeep?" Penny thought she saw Audrey's eyes darken just a little.

"Oh no! Not at all. In fact I had to tell him to leave. He came by late yesterday afternoon and was so drunk he could hardly stand up. He was quite obnoxious, in fact." She paused. "It is embarrassing really, we met online. I thought we may have some things in common but as it turned out he was not who I thought he was. I have learned my lesson," she laughed. "No more online dating for me."

Poppy turned off the jets on the spa so they didn't have to shout at each other. She had some questions for Audrey. "You must have been quite frightened here during all those murders. I read some of the bodies were found on your own beaches and some of the perpetrators actually stayed here at Tiromoana." As soon as Poppy asked the questions, she knew she was treading on thin ice.

Audrey reached again for her glass and took a sip before responding. "Owning a property like this in rural isolation tends to attract the wrong people. I try to vet who stays here, but it's impossible to know for sure." She returned her glass slowly to the side of the spa and looked at Penny with cold green eyes. "You have been doing a lot of reading about the area, I see."

"Oh nothing much. Mostly trying to find out what are the hot spots for dining, boating, fishing and socializing. It just came up in conversation that Tiromoana has been a focal point in many of the crimes in the area. I was just curious, that's all."

"You don't have to worry. It is only fish the guests are after here," Audrey laughed.

Poppy was beginning to feel quite woozy after drinking all afternoon and the hot tub was not making her feel any better. "I think I had better get some sleep." She stepped out of the spa and dried herself off. "I should have an early night. It has been a busy day."

Audrey joined her on the deck. "Looks like rain tonight. Thanks for your company."

Poppy watched her leave, wrapped in a towel and carrying her half full bottle. She didn't look like a murderer. In fact she looked quite harmless. But her eyes were a give-away. Her eyes were cold. Penny shivered. Audrey was good. She now understood why no-one ever suspected her of the crimes. But Poppy knew otherwise. And before she left Tiromoana, Audrey Wetherby would be locked up. She had no doubt about that.

CHAPTER 21

The rain continued all night and into the morning light. Audrey awoke sensing danger. She wondered if she should check the Jeep's location. The stench of the dead body should be potent. The trackers usually worked midweek. It was less than forty-eight hours since Grant Pratt had taken his last breath. She hoped nature had taken its course. A body left out in the open decomposed a lot faster than in the ground. Insects, maggots and even animals helped the process.

Audrey put on her gumboots, raincoat and headed off up Peninsula Road. She saw the trackers heading into the property next door. They had their base hut there. She hoped they were not setting traps further up the peninsula. Audrey had yet to meet her new neighbor who had moved in a few months ago. He lived there alone, she had heard.

She saw them when she turned the next bend – a couple. She wondered if they were from the Motor Camp. Often tourists walked up the rural gravel road in hope of finding access to the beaches below. There wasn't. The road just meandered up the hill and came to a dead end a few miles up. A handful of holiday homes were hidden deep into the bush on either side of the road with long winding driveways creating even more seclusion. She wondered why a couple would be walking in the rain. She hastened her pace hoping to pass them. The Jeep was quite a distance up the road. She hoped they would not be venturing too far in the rain.

They were an odd couple. Could have been father and daughter except he was Caucasian and she was obviously one hundred percent, Asian. Audrey had a personal and hardened hatred toward old men bringing over young Asian brides. Just another form of legalized prostitution in her mind. She wrapped her scarf around her face and pulled her hood down in order to disguise herself as she greeted the couple with a short "Hello." Gathering speed she quickly turned the next corner and out of sight of the oddly paired couple.

She could smell him from the road. Strong, decaying meat. She had lost one of her sheep a few years ago down the bank and the smell was similar. She had asked a strange gentleman on his stroll if he had seen her pet ram. He had pointed to the curve in the road ahead and said he smelled something rotting down the bank.

She wondered if the couple would venture this far up the road. Surely not? The rain was getting heavier. She turned back towards Tiromoana and passed the couple who luckily had also decided to turn back. She doubted the trappers would venture out past their base hut in the rain. The location of Mr. Pratt's body would be secure for at least another twenty-four hours.

CHAPTER 22

Mei was horrified. What had she done? What was she thinking? The man was old, too old. She didn't know how she was going to get to her studies from such an isolated place. The house was big, cold and empty. The grey, swollen ocean looked angry. The rain drenched the surrounding bush. She had agreed to take a walk up the peninsula with the man. She just wanted to get out of the house but the rain became so heavy the man wanted to return home and light the fire.

She sat in the big armchair watching the man stoke the fire. He was fat. There was no doubt about that, fat and short. Mei was brought up to value qualities in a man other than his physical appearance. Security and family were far more important. Mei knew this man could provide security but it was unlikely he could provide a family. She wondered if he wanted to have children. She shuddered at the thought of being intimate with him. Last night had been difficult. She had hoped they would have separate bedrooms until they were married. The man, however, was adamant they share the same bed. Mei was alone with the man. She had no choice. Her thin nightgown was no protection from his advances. His heavy rotund body and beery breath were repulsive to her. He kissed her roughly with his open wet mouth, leaving spit on her face. Rough fat hands cupped her small breasts as they made their way down to her private parts. His rough fingers penetrated her in the attempt to moisten her dry rebellion. He took her small hand and placed it on his limp, soft penis and told her to make him hard. It was everything she wished it wasn't. Thank goodness his desires were quickly satisfied and he fell on his back and within minutes was snoring loudly into the night. She lay there looking at the high white ceiling for a long time. She must leave this place. But where could she go? She knew no-one in New Zealand. Her parents were not wealthy. She had lied about that. They were ordinary working people and had used all their savings to send her to school in New Zealand. She could not dishonor them by returning so soon. She must come up with a plan. She could not stay here.

CHAPTER 23

Audrey watched Poppy drive away from her cabin at noon and knew she must do a little investigation. Was Poppy who she said she was? She used her master key to enter the cabin. It was immaculate. Her computer sat on the table surrounded by brochures from various motels, restaurants, boat charters, bush walks and various other holiday attractions. She turned on the computer and was surprised there was no password required. A quick check of her files and email revealed nothing other than Poppy was starting up a new online tourist business. She turned off the computer and checked out her closet. Nice clothes, expensive clothes. She opened up drawers and neatly checked their contents. Nothing interesting. Poppy must be who she said she is. She made sure everything was in it place and left the cabin. But the feeling that something was wrong stayed with her. A warning? A premonition? She didn't know. But something wasn't' right.

Returning to the office she was greeted by Detective Inspector Bromley. "Afternoon Audrey. Got a minute?"

"Why Detective, this is a surprise. It has been quite a long time since we last met. I hear congratulations are in order. You are an Inspector now."

"Thank you. Yes. I'm still getting used to it."

"Just a friendly visit or can I help you with something?"

"Actually, yes. I understand a Grant Pratt was staying here on Saturday night. His friends back home have not heard from him and apparently he borrowed one of their vehicles. They have filed a missing person's report and, as your place was his last known location, I was wondering if you knew where he went when he left here?"

Shit! Shit! Shit! Audrey hadn't expected his absence to surface so soon. "I have to be honest with you, Detective. Mr. Pratt and I had been corresponding via a dating service. I invited him up last Saturday for lunch. Unfortunately I did not know Mr. Pratt was a heavy drinker and when I invited him to stay for dinner, he over indulged in the wine and was unable to drive back to Thames. I put him up in the Morepork Cabin, so he could sleep it off."

"And the next day? What time did he leave?"

"It must have been late morning. I am not sure. One of my guests, Poppy Perkins, came into the office as I was insisting he leave. She overheard our discussion I am sure. He was not happy. In fact he was pretty pissed off if I may say so."

"And you didn't see him again?"

"I wish I hadn't. Instead of leaving, he must have stayed locally somewhere and spent the next day drinking. He arrived here about four o'clock on Monday afternoon, completely drunk and obnoxious. We argued for some time and finally I got him to leave. It was quite frightening. He wasn't at all who I thought he was. He was so drunk when he left I presume he would have gone somewhere and slept in his car."

"And you never heard from him again?"

"Thank goodness. No."

"A Bob Stark said he spoke to you about his friend being missing."

"Oh yes. I explained to him that as far as I knew he was returning home."

"What time did he leave on Monday night?" "You know, I don't even remember. It was still light. I was just pleased to see him go."

"And you say your guest, Poppy Perkins, heard you arguing with Mr. Pratt? Is she still staying here?"

"Yes, she has booked in for a few weeks. Setting up a new travel business."

"Do you know if she is in?"

"No, I saw her drive away about thirty minutes ago. You just missed her."

"If you see her, can you ask her to give me a call?"

Audrey watched the detective leave up her driveway and shut the door. Damn! She listened to hear which way his car headed. She held her breath until she heard his wheels crunching on the gravel as he headed down the hill towards the Hihi Township.

Audrey knew she had some time before the police would suspect anything. After all, now they knew his whereabouts on Monday night. It could easily take a couple of days for him to return to Thames especially as he was a heavy drinker and there were a number of pubs on the way. She heard a car. It was Poppy returning. She made her way to her cabin to pass on the detective's message.

CHAPTER 24

I t was always the same crowd in the Mangonui Pub in the afternoon. The Mangonui women were community minded with time on their hands. They volunteered at the visitor's center, the Community Library and the Art Gallery. Their husbands fished, boated and shared stories with their mates at the pub. It was a friendly place with an obvious absence of female patronage. Even the slot machines in the back room were male operated. The pool table was not in use and the local crowd were leaning on the bar chatting to the owner when Constable Inspector Bromley walked in.

He received a warm welcome from his neighbors. "Detective, come for a beer?" the owner asked.

"Sorry. On duty."

"What can we do for you?"

"I don't suppose you remember a tall, lanky guy, Grant Pratt, who may have been in here on Monday?" the detective asked.

"From Thames?" one of the guys asked.

"Yes, you remember him?" The detective was surprised.

"Quite a drinker, he was. Said he was up visiting a friend."

"Do you know what time he left here?"

"It was late in the afternoon. Don't know what time."

The others all nodded their heads in agreement.

"He was pretty sloshed when he left. I remember thinking I hope he isn't driving very far. I doubt if he would have made it back to Thames in his condition," the owner said, "In fact, I suggested he stay in the village that night. I don't know if he took my advice."

Bromley thanked the guys and walked outside to discover the rain had stopped and the afternoon sun was working diligently to dry away the drops and puddles left by the spring shower.

On his way back to the station his phone rang. It was Poppy. He was pleased. He had been thinking of her constantly. He had hoped to see her at Tiromoana. He wanted to see her again, smell her, laugh with her, look into those mesmerizing eyes of hers.

"Poppy. How are you?" he said. He could hear her smiling. She liked to tease him.

"Inspector, I hear you were looking for me. Miss me already?"

"It's all business," he found himself explaining. "Where are you?"

"I am back at Tiromoana. Just popped out for some supplies. Why?"

"I have some questions for you. Do you have a moment?"

Poppy sat down at the table and poured herself a glass of fresh orange juice. "Go ahead. I'm all ears."

Bromley steered his car into the parking area outside the station and turned off the engine. "I am looking into a missing person case, a Grant Pratt. He stayed at Tiromoana on Saturday night. On Sunday morning, apparently Audrey and he had a disagreement. Audrey mentioned that you might have overheard their discussion."

"A Grant Pratt, you say?" Poppy wrote down the name on the pad beside her computer. "Do you know what he looks like?"

"I have a photo of him. Do you want me to email it through to you?"

"Yes. That would be great." She gave him her email address and asked, "Can you describe him anyway?"

"He is a tall, lean man in his late 50s. Ring any bells?"

"Ah, yes. I do remember him. In fact, I saw Audrey and this Mr. Pratt walking down to Rocky Beach on Saturday. I also heard them arguing on Sunday morning. He was not happy to be leaving. Seems as though he had expected to stay longer. Audrey was insistent that he leave."

"Audrey said he returned on Monday at four o'clock and left a couple of hours later. He was drunk and she had trouble getting him to leave. I don't suppose you saw him or heard anything that might corroborate her story?"

Poppy couldn't believe her luck. A missing man! Audrey's involved. She was part of the investigation. It couldn't be better for her book. "I did hear a man's voice about that time. I went over to Audrey's to suggest she join me for a drink and when I heard the man's raised voice, I left and didn't even knock. I did see his Jeep leave about six o'clock or around that time."

"Thanks Poppy. It seems as though Mr. Pratt was pretty intoxicated when he left Tiromoana. It was only a couple of days ago and chances are he is still on his way back to Thames. I'll let his friends know. If he doesn't turn up in a day or two, I might have more questions."

"So that's it?" she teased.

Bromley didn't know how to answer. Of course he didn't want it left there. But he had no right to expect Poppy Perkins may want to see him again. He was a married man. He must remember that.

"That's it." He replied. "I'll send through the photo of Pratt anyway just for confirmation."

"O.K. If I learn anything more, I'll let you know."

Bromley opened the door to the car and made his way into the station. He forwarded Pratt's photo to Poppy. Somehow just having her email address seemed like a gift, a way to communicate. He knew he was treading a fine line. He texted: 'Poppy, nice talking with you. Let me know if you remember anything more regarding Pratt.' He pressed 'send' then regretted *the nice talking with you* part. Too personal. Damn!

He called Bob Stark. "Mr. Stark, Detective Inspector Bromley here. Just wanted to follow up regarding your friend, Grant Pratt. Apparently, he was seen here on Monday evening. Left Hihi about six o'clock presumably on his way back to Thames. I take it Pratt is a bit of a boozer. Spent Monday at the local pub here. Pretty wasted when he left. Must have stopped to sleep it off somewhere. My guess is he taking his time. Let me know if he doesn't return in a day or two and I'll do some more checking.

CHAPTER 25

Poppy was so excited she could hardly contain herself. She wanted to run over to Audrey's office and ask her about the disappearance of her friend, Grant Pratt. She wished she had asked the detective for more details. Had Audrey made him disappear? Why were they arguing so vehemently?

Poppy had left a few small traps around the cabin in order to see if Audrey had taken her bait and done some snooping. She wasn't disappointed. Her drawers had been opened, her suitcase checked, her computer had been used and even the clothes in her wardrobe had been sorted through. Poppy took this intrusion as a sign of Audrey's obvious guilt. Why else would she be prying into her personal space?

Poppy opened up her computer and inserted her memory stick. Something was familiar about the man's disappearance. Then she remembered the man's body that was found up Peninsula Road in his car a few years ago. Suicide, they said. Poppy thought otherwise.

She read through the newspaper archives and wondered if Audrey had disposed of this Mr. Pratt the same way.

She snapped shut her laptop and grabbed her jacket. She might just take a walk up there anyway. What the heck! She could do with a walk. And the rain had stopped.

The road was still wet from the rain. It meandered around bends thickly lined with pine, gum and tea trees. Huge punga fronds protruded over banks and bush. The fresh smell of rain still clung to their branches. Poppy breathed in the cool, crisp spring air as she quickened her pace and headed up the Peninsula.

The stench was overwhelming. At first she thought it was a dead possum or weasel caught in a trap and left to rot but as she approached the area, the smell became overpowering. A sheep maybe, or a dog having eaten poison left by the Trappers. Curiosity was stronger than caution and Poppy made her way down the steep bank in search of the culprit. It was a long way down the bank. She couldn't see anything but gorse, bush, branches and heavy overgrowth. It was slippery from the rain and she found herself slipping in the mud. Branches tore at her hair, face and hands. She slipped constantly. This is stupid! I should just go back. There is nothing here.

It looked like rusted metal. Twisted, bent pieces. A door, bumper – just pieces. Poppy realized it was just an old car obviously dumped here a while ago. Then she saw the 'Jeep' logo and realized it could be Grant Pratt's old Jeep. She could hardly breathe. Too scared to get closer but drawn to the sight – she just stood there. Looking at what could be a crime scene. She felt in her pocket for her cell phone, removed it and started to take photos. It was difficult to get a clear shot. The bush was thick, and vines wrapped their roots like rope between the trees. Squeezing through their barrier, she slowly made her way further down the bank to the Jeep. It had literally fallen apart leaving car parts strewn in all directions. Then she saw it - a body, swollen, unrecognizable, crawling with bugs and maggots and half eaten by rodents. The stench was unbearable. The scene was horrific. She lifted her phone and began to take more photos. Should she call the detective?

Poppy felt she now had an ownership in this crime. And she was sure it was a crime. Two bodies found on the same remote road. Both men had stayed at Tiromoana. There had to be a connection between the two cases, and she was pretty sure it was Audrey Wetherby.

The smell forced her to retrace her steps up the bank and back onto the road. As she headed back to her cabin, she felt elated, alive, excited. She would decide when she returned and had had a glass of wine, what she would do with this information. For now, she was the only one who knew what lay at the bottom of the cliff. Well, her and the killer, Audrey Wetherby. Now they shared a secret.

CHAPTER 26

Audrey watched Poppy walking up the ridge towards her cabin. She looked disheveled as though she had been fighting her way through scrub and bush. Audrey called out to her. "Been for a walk? It's so nice now the rain has gone."

"Oh just a quick walk to get some fresh air."

Audrey returned to her office. She smelled trouble. Poppy was trouble. What was she up to? Had she been for a walk up the road? Had she found Grant's body? No. She can't have. She was too calm. She would have been panicking, calling the Police. Could she risk it?

Audrey picked up some fresh towels and made her way over to Poppy's cabin. A quick knock at the door and she was face to face with someone she realized was hiding a secret. It was written all over Poppy's face. Audrey recognized it. A sense of excitement, anticipation, fear of exposure - all wrapped into one, marvelous feeling of power. She knew. Poppy knew. Audrey didn't know how or why she was choosing to remain silent but there was no doubt she knew. Had she found the body? Yes, that was it.

"Just brought over some clean towels. Do you have any towels that need laundering? "Audrey watched her smile and casually reply.

"Thanks no, nothing at the moment," Poppy took the clean towels and politely closed the door.

Audrey was fucked. She knew it. There was nothing she could do except return to the cottage and wait. She couldn't risk moving the body, as the police were most likely on their way to the location now. Plus, the car couldn't be moved. It would look like he was drunk and driven off the hill. She forced herself to stop worrying. She had covered her tracks. Even if Poppy Perkins suspected she was involved, she would need proof.

Audrey had to do an online search. It was time to find out exactly who this woman was.

In just a few seconds a photo of Poppy and an article from the New Zealand Herald, a couple of years ago, appeared on the screen:

Sister of dead investigator, Poppy Perkins, returns from Australia to attend her brother's funeral held in the Auckland Memorial Funeral Home on Friday. Miss Perkins is a well-known journalist in Australia and was horrified to hear of her brother's death.

Shit! Shit! Shit! She's the private investigator's sister! They don't even share the same name.

"Private Investigator, Eric Chapman, was found dead at his home on the North Shore at ten o'clock this morning. The police are treating his death as a possible homicide. It was

Mr. Chapman who found Detective Constable Higgins'
body only last Tuesday in Hihi Bay where they were
reported to be on a fishing trip.

That is why she is here. She is here because of her brother. But why has she not called the police? They would have been here by now. Audrey picked up a bottle of wine and headed back to Poppy's cabin. If Poppy let her in, it could only be one thing - she suspected Audrey of her brother's death and time was of the essence.

CHAPTER 27

Mei was miserable. All day he just sat by the fire and watched her work. He checked everything she did and made suggestions as to how she could improve with her housekeeping chores. She was not familiar with what he called *good ol' Kiwi tucker*. She just knew he would not eat *Chink* food. Which she presumed meant Chinese food. After dinner she asked if he would mind if she could take a walk. He just grunted. She took that as a 'yes' and removed her jacket from the peg inside the front door, donned her walking boots and headed up Peninsula Road.

It was a beautiful evening. Steve liked to eat early so the sun was still reasonably high in the sky. She was surprised no-one was around. Steve had mentioned that soon the owners of properties further up the road would be returning for the summer. It felt wonderful to be alone. It had been a mistake coming here. As she turned the next corner there was an awful odor. It smelled like death. A dead animal, she guessed. The smell was so bad she wondered if she should find out what it was. It could be one of Steve's cows and he would want to know.

She climbed down the bank until she reached pieces of metal from a vehicle, which looked as though it had careered down the bank. Mei was a sensible girl. Not known to be faint of heart when it came to an emergency. She saw the body and realized whoever it was had died from the crash. She was a visitor to this country and not comfortable getting involved with the police. She didn't know if she should tell Steve about what she had seen. He might be annoyed with her for getting involved. Mei climbed back up the bank and headed towards her new home. Maybe she should forget what she saw. Someone else will find the body and call the police she was sure of it.

It was almost dark before Mei returned to the big house on the hill. The man was angry. He had been drinking and demanded to know why she had taken so long. Mei had no choice, she told the man what she had seen.

CHAPTER 28

Poppy saw her approaching the cabin with a bottle of wine in her hand. *She's got balls.* "Audrey, what a surprise."

"Such a nice evening. Thought you might like to share a bottle of wine."

"Why not? Great idea. Come in."

Poppy watched Audrey pour out two glasses of wine and waited for her to take the first sip. "So, I hear your friend, Grant Pratt has gone missing."

Audrey didn't miss a beat. "Yes, Detective Inspector Bromley was here earlier today enquiring about him. I told him he was here early Monday evening making a nuisance of himself. He finally left and I presumed he was heading back to Thames. He was pretty wasted. Not a nice guy."

"Had you known him for long?"

"No, not at all. We only just became acquainted. I told the detective you had seen him in my office and overheard our quarrel the other day. I presume he got in touch with you?"

"Yes, he called me."

"So how is your travel business going?"

"Oh great. Getting lots of work done."

"I would love to see your website. Do you have it up and running?"

Poppy walked over to her laptop on the table and placed it on the coffee table between them. Audrey removed the glasses to make more room.

"Brilliant. Love it!" complimented Audrey. "I do a lot of my marketing online." Let's take our drinks outside and enjoy the evening.

Poppy picked up her glass and they walked outside to the lounge chairs on the deck. She had such an exhausting day and it was getting the better of her. As she finished her second glass she realized she just couldn't keep her eyes open. She looked over at Audrey in the other chair. She had her eyes closed. The tuis were singing in the big gum tree on the edge of the ridge. The waves lapped against the rocks in distance. Poppy closed her eyes.

CHAPTER 29

Audrey waited until she was sure Poppy was fast asleep. She had given her just enough GHB to knock her out for a couple of hours - enough time to check out what Miss Perkins knew.

Walking inside she found Poppy's cell phone on the table. Putting on gloves, she quickly checked her messages. She had been in touch with Detective Inspector Bromley all right. By the looks of it they had been communicating from the day she arrived. She wondered what they had to talk about so many times. Then she saw her photo folder. Fuck! She scanned through photo after photo of the crash scene. The Jeep, Grant's bloated body, everything. She returned the phone to the table.

Finding Poppy's car keys, she searched the contents of the car and the trunk but found nothing interesting. The laptop was still full of benign information. A cover story, Audrey suspected. There was only one more place to search: Poppy's pockets. She found it, a memory stick, tucked in a pocket of her jacket hanging on the peg by the door. She inserted it into Poppy's computer and it confirmed what she already knew. Poppy believed Audrey was responsible for the murder of her brother. She was also in the process of trying to link all the local murders to Audrey. The files showed enough evidence that Poppy was obsessed with proving Audrey was a murderer. The photos she had taken of the crash site were also on the memory stick. She copied the relevant files and photos to her own memory stick and returned the original to Poppy's jacket pocket.

Poppy's obsession would be her weakness. If the police suspect Grant Pratt's death was a murder, she had proof Poppy wanted to frame her for the crime. Why else wouldn't she call the police immediately upon finding the body?

Audrey just had one small task to take care of. Taking one of Poppy's silk scarfs she made a very quick trip to the crash site in Poppy's car. She pulled the car close to the edge of the road so the tires left indents in the damp ground. She left the scarf jammed between the driver's seat and the passenger's seat. At least what was left of them. As she drove back towards Tiromoana, she saw a young woman on foot about to turn into her neighbor's driveway. Audrey was pleased it was almost dark. The last thing she needed was to be seen driving Poppy's car.

With everything in its place Audrey returned to the lounge chair on the deck and closed her eyes. The sun had already set when Poppy awoke.

"We fell asleep. Can you believe it?" Poppy looked over at Audrey.

Audrey yawned. "Oh it was so peaceful. I haven't slept that well in ages." She laughed. "Oh, look at the time, I must be going."

She picked up both glasses and headed inside to the kitchen where she gave them a good wash and placed them to dry on the bench. As she was about to leave, the sound of sirens screaming up Peninsula Road shattered the isolated silence.

"I wonder what's causing all the excitement?" said Poppy, as she picked up her cell phone and checked for messages.

"I wonder," said Audrey.

CHAPTER 30

Detective Inspector Bromley was working late at the station when the call came in. A body has been seen at an accident site in Hihi. A local resident made the call. The resident was waiting on Peninsula Road where a Jeep had veered off the road and was at the bottom of a cliff.

"Steve Sutton," the man introduced himself. He pointed the detective inspector and the other police to the area where the Jeep had careered off the road and down the bank. "My fiancé was taking a walk up here earlier tonight and could smell something dead. She thought it might be one of our cows and climbed down the bank to check it out."

The police scrambled down the bank with spotlights and ropes.

"Down here," one of the policemen called out. "Looks like the driver's been dead for a few days."

Bromley quickly scrambled down the bank to the site. The stench of death was overwhelming. He quickly realized he knew who the driver was. It was Grant Pratt. He recognized the plate number as the missing Jeep.

"I know who he is," he told the others. "Forensics should be here soon. Don't touch a thing. We don't know the cause of the accident, or if it was an accident."

"Quite a few broken bottles of beer around the area," commented a young constable.

Bromley recognized the area. This was close to the site where the killer of the teen prostitute was found dead in his car, with his gun at his side. Another death in Hihi. He knew from his conversation with Audrey Wetherby, the man had been pretty drunk when he left her place on Monday evening. By the look of the body he had not got far. But why go uphill? The road led nowhere. If he was going to sleep in his car surely he would have headed downhill to the Hihi township. Did he just make the wrong turn?

After forensics had checked the body, they made a joint decision to rope off the area and remove the body and the Jeep in the morning, when it was light and they could get the right equipment to the site.

When Bromley returned home it was well after mid-night. It had been a long night and he had to be back at the accident site first thing in the morning.

It would be a busy day.

CHAPTER 31

Poppy had a dilemma. Should she tell Detective Inspector Bromley she had found the body yesterday or keep quiet? He would wonder why she had not called him to report the accident. If she said nothing, Audrey might get away with murder.

Her plan had really backfired on her. She was hoping to have more proof of Audrey's guilt before going to the police. At the moment, she had nothing.

Last night had been rather strange. She usually didn't fall asleep during the day. She guessed she had been overdoing it lately. Staying up late researching old cases, not sleeping well, seeing a dead body and entertaining a murderer – no wonder she was stressed and tired.

She turned on the morning news and it was the lead story.

"A body of a man identified as Grant Pratt has been found in Hihi. At this time the police are considering his death an accident. The Jeep he was driving careered off a steep gravel road into a gully thirty meters below."

An accident, like hell! Poppy knew Audrey was going to get

away with murder again. She had heard them arguing that night. Maybe it wasn't Mr. Pratt who drove the Jeep away that night. What if it was Audrey and she took him to the site in the middle of the night. She had heard a car coming and going in the early hours. Poppy opened her laptop, inserted her memory stick and began to write her theory.

When her phone rang, she was surprised it was Detective Inspector Bromley.

"Poppy, I guess you have heard we have found Grant Pratt's body up the road from you. Forensics is still working at the scene. I am just returning to the station, thought I would pop by on the way past. Are you going to be around?"

"Yes, I am here. Just working. See you soon."

She watched as his car pulled up in front of her cabin. He was an attractive man. What a shame he was married. She opened the door and offered him a cold drink.

"Thanks," he accepted the cold glass of orange juice and joined her at the table. "Working on your book?"

"Yes, I didn't expect another murder to take place so soon."

"Murder? I think you are jumping the gun a little, don't you think?"

"Of course it was murder. I heard Audrey and the man arguing the night he went missing. I also heard a car in the early hours of the morning coming and going. Isn't that the same place that the man shot himself after killing that teen girl?"

"Yes, in the same area. But that was suicide. This was an accident."

"All I can say is, make sure you do an autopsy."

Bromley's phone rang. "I have to get this," he said.

Poppy watched as he walked outside to his car. She heard him say, "I am just ten minutes away." He saw her watching him and waved as he backed out and took off in haste.

CHAPTER 32

Detective Inspector Bromley looked at the photo of the pale blue scarf found in the Jeep. Forensics were checking it for DNA. He had seen that scarf before, around the beautiful neck of Poppy Perkins. How the hell did it get in the Jeep? Surely it is not the same scarf. But his gut told him it was exactly the same scarf. It had small shell shapes on the trim. He remembered everything about their afternoon on the boat together. Poppy had never mentioned being in Mr. Pratt's Jeep or even knowing him personally. He would wait until the DNA results came in.

He checked his inbox and saw the coroners, report on Pratt. There was no doubt he was highly intoxicated at the time of death. Four times the legal limit. The report also stated he could have been suffocated. There were tiny burst blood vessels in his eyes. But this was difficult to confirm due to the condition of the body. He would have to wait until forensics completed their report before coming to any conclusion as to the real cause of death.

He looked up as Audrey Wetherby entered the foyer of the

station. He walked out to meet her. "Audrey, what can I do for you?"

"Do you have a moment, Inspector? I would like to talk to you."

"Yes, yes. Come into my office."

"I don't know how to say this. I have come across some information regarding the death of Grant Pratt and it has made me very uncomfortable. In fact, I am quite frightened. I thought the only thing to do was to talk to you."

Bromley could tell Audrey was upset. He had never seen her so afraid. "What is it? "

Audrey leaned forward on her chair as if someone might hear her and spoke softly. "I have found out something about my guest, Poppy Perkins. She is the sister of the private investigator, Eric Chapman, who was found dead in his home a couple of years ago. Over the past few days I have been getting strange vibes from her. She told me she was setting up a travel business but I have found out she is writing a true crime novel and I am the main perpetrator in the book. She suspects me of carrying out every murder that ever happened from Auckland to Northland. She is obsessed with it."

Bromley was shocked. Eric Chapman's sister! Poppy had never mentioned this fact. "How do you know all this?" he asked.

"I know I shouldn't have, but I decided to check her computer when she was not there one day." She handed him a memory stick.

Bromley inserted the stick into his computer and opened up the files.

"Check the photo files first." Audrey prompted.

"Bloody Hell! These are photos of Grant Pratt's accident scene."

"She has been writing about how she wants to frame me for

his accident. If she found his body, why didn't she call the police?"

"Leave this with me. You did the right thing by reporting this. I will let you know if I need a statement. The fact that you had no legal right to take this information from her computer means we cannot use this information in court. But, Miss Perkins definitely has some explaining to do."

"Thank you, Inspector. I'll leave it with you then." Audrey stood, picked up her bag, and left his office.

Bromley was so busy looking at the photos on his screen he didn't even see her go.

Fuck! Now what? Bromley sat back on his chair and stretched his legs. Damn it! He knew she was too good to be true.

CHAPTER 33

Poppy was in heaven. She had already finished her first three chapters. This new murder was just too good to believe. She had heard the argument, seen the Jeep drive away, heard a car in the early hours of the morning, which she was sure was Audrey disposing of the body and creating a false accident scene, now she just had to prove it. She looked at the photos from the scene of the accident. I have you now, Audrey.

It was after midday when her cell phone beeped indicating a message. It was from Detective Inspector Bromley asking her to come into the station to answer some questions. What questions? Did they suspect Audrey already? Yes!

Where was her blue scarf? She had only packed a limited wardrobe for her stay and her scarf was a staple. It went with everything. She looked high and low and thought she may have left it in the inspector's boat. That was the last time she had worn it. She must ask him if he had seen it. She chose black tights and a tunic sweater and, checking her reflection in the full-length mirror, went off to meet her admirer.

As Poppy headed down the long driveway she saw a young Asian girl walking up the drive towards the cabins. The girl waved at her and smiled. She waved back. She turned on the radio and sang all the way to the Mangonui Police station.

CHAPTER 34

Audrey was surprised to see a young Asian girl knocking at her cottage door. It was early afternoon and she had just finished checking her new guests into their cabins. Not having heard or seen a car she wondered if the girl had walked to Tiromoana.

"Hello. Are you looking for accommodation?" she asked the girl.

"Oh no. I live next door. I am Steve Sutton's fiancé, Mei Wong."

"Oh. Come in," Audrey welcomed her inside. "I have not met your fiancé yet. I feel rather guilty. He has been living there for a few months now. We all tend to keep to ourselves here. How long have you been living there?"

"Just a few days."

Audrey noticed the girl looked upset. "Is something wrong?" she asked. "Can I help you?"

"I saw the body," she said.

"What body?"

"The man's body, down the cliff. It was awful. I told Steve and he called the police."

"How did you come to see the body?"

"I went for a walk and could smell something funny. I climbed down the bank and saw the man lying there. I didn't know what to do.

"That is awful. What you need is a nice hot cup of tea."

Audrey soon realized the poor girl knew nobody and was obviously not happy with her choice to come to New Zealand. "So you have come here to study?" she asked.

"Yes, but Steve said I cannot go to the school in Auckland and have to do my studies online. But my courses are not available online. "

"I don't understand. Why agree to marry someone who lives up here in Northland if you want to live in Auckland and study there."

"It was my parents. They cannot afford to pay for me here. I agreed to marry so I could study here. Now I don't want to get married. Steve is an old man. I am not happy here."

Audrey immediately disliked this Steve guy.

What a shit. Bringing over such a sweet young girl. She must be no older than twenty, if that. "Maybe you could call your parents and ask if you can return home."

"That would bring shame to my family."

Audrey knew she could not help Mei. "I'm sorry Mei. I don't know what I can do to help. But feel free to come over here for a chat now and then."

"I saw the lady who drives that nice car again. She was coming down the hill after I found the dead man. Are there other people living up Peninsula Road? Steve said there is no-one living there until summer."

Audrey smiled. She had seen her driving Poppy's car and thought it was Poppy. Perfect.

"It is always quiet this time of year," she replied. "Most of the houses are holiday houses. There are just a few of us that live here year-round."

As she watched poor sad little Mei leaving down the drive she realized she now had a witness.

CHAPTER 35

He observed her entering the lobby of the station. Beautiful, as always. Her perfume was familiar now. "Poppy, thanks for coming in." He led her into an office at the back of the station. He had no idea how this interview was going to go and didn't want to attract the attention of the constable working in the front office.

"You haven't seen my pale blue scarf, have you? I think I may have left it on your boat? I have looked everywhere for it."

Shit! It is her scarf. "You didn't leave it on the boat," he said.

"So, this is all really exciting. Have you got information regarding Grant Pratt's accident? Was it murder?"

"We need to talk, Poppy," the inspector became serious. "I have some questions for you."

"It sounds important. What is it?" Poppy began to feel a little uncomfortable. The inspector seemed distracted. He was looking at something on his computer.

"It has come to my attention you were at the accident scene prior to the police being informed. Can you tell me why you were there?"

How could he possibly know I was there? "What makes you think I was there?" Poppy avoided answering the question.

"It is better you tell the truth, Poppy."

Poppy felt trapped. "What do you know?"

"I know you were at the scene."

The inspector turned his laptop around so Poppy could look at the photo of the screen. Her scarf jammed between the two front seats of the Jeep. She recognized it immediately. She knew he had recognized it too. Poppy's mind was spinning. She was sure she was not wearing the scarf the day she went up Peninsula Road. How did it get there? Audrey?

"If it is my scarf, I never put it there," was all she could say.

"I think we both know it is your scarf. The question is, how did it end up in Grant Pratt's Jeep? Have you been in his Jeep?"

"I didn't even know Grant Pratt!" Poppy was indignant. "He was Audrey's friend. I bet it was Audrey who planted my scarf in the Jeep."

"She said you would say that."

"She said what? You have been talking to her about this?"

"Audrey came into the station earlier today. She feels you are trying to frame her for Grant Pratt's accident. She has discovered why you are really staying at her cabins. She knows you are writing a true crime book about the murders in the area. She feels you are obsessed with making her the perpetrator of the crimes."

Poppy felt her face redden. She had no idea Audrey was on to her.

"What's more," continued the inspector "she told me you are Eric Chapman's sister. Why didn't you confide in me Poppy?"

"I am sure Audrey had something to do with my brother's death."

"I could have told you she had nothing to do with it. She was in Hihi and he was in Auckland when he died. She could not have possibly been involved in his death."

Poppy realized she was in trouble. "Am I a suspect in Grant Pratt's death?"

"I need to know why you were at the crime scene?" He looked at Poppy waiting for her to confess. He had proof. Photos from her camera. Details of the crime written in detail in her manuscript.

"Am I under arrest?" Poppy stood to leave.

"No. You are free to go." He tried once more. "Poppy, I don't understand, why won't you just tell me why you were at the crime scene?"

"I suspected Audrey might have disposed of Grant Pratt the same way she disposed of the guy who killed the teenage prostitute. He was found in almost the same location. They said it was suicide. I believe she killed him. It was just a gut instinct. I went to the same location that night to see if I was right. And I was. That is how I found the crime scene. I should have called you straight away. I didn't. I don't know why." Poppy was near tears. "I thought I could trap Audrey somehow. Make her confess."

"I see," said the inspector. "By doing that you have contaminated the crime scene. If it even is a crime scene. The man was drunk. He went over the bank. Go home Poppy. I will contact you if I have more questions."

Poppy stood to go.

"How did your scarf end up in the Jeep?"

"Audrey put it there."

"Poppy, Audrey hasn't even been to the crime scene."

"And you believe her?"

He knew he would have to talk to her again. Poppy had no idea he had copies of the photos she took of Grant Pratt's body and the wrecked Jeep.

When Poppy left the station Bromley checked her photos again. Something was bothering him. He pulled up the photo of the Jeep. That was it. There was no scarf in the photo. How did it get there? When? And by whom?

CHAPTER 36

S teve Sutton was dissatisfied with his choice of women. This girl was a feisty little thing who was stubborn and far too independent for his liking. She would wander off and not say a word. Now it was all over the neighborhood he had a young Asian woman living with him. Stupid girl wandering off and finding that man's body. The police were asking questions. Steve Sutton had a history. A history he preferred no-one to know about. Now he had the police nosing around. Why she had to go climbing down the bank that day he couldn't fathom.

He saw Mei walking into the house, removing her muddy shoes and hanging her coat on the peg by the door. "Where 'ya been this time?" he asked her as she made her way into the kitchen.

"I have been visiting Audrey next door. She has a good business there. The gardens are very nice. She gave me some cuttings from her succulents." Mei placed a handful of plants into a jug of water and, keeping her back turned, she dared to confront him with her situation. "Audrey believes I really need to study in

Auckland. I don't think this is a good idea me staying here in Hihi. It is too isolated and I would prefer to live in the city."

"So this Audrey has been putting ideas into your pretty head!" Steve was furious. "We have an arrangement. Your parents agreed to this arrangement. What would they say if you told them that just after a couple of days you have decided to break our agreement? You answer me that!"

Mei hung her head. This is the hardest thing she had ever had to do in her whole life but she knew she had no choice. She couldn't marry this short, fat man who was unkind and unloving. He was old and ugly and mean. "I will find a job in Auckland and pay my own way," she said quietly.

"And what sort of job could you possibly get?"

"I don't know."

"You couldn't even get a job as a whore. You have no experience. But, if you are so sure you want to leave. Then go! Get out of here! Don't expect me to drive you anywhere. Why don't you get your new friend, Audrey to help you? You will soon come running back. It is a cruel world out there."

Mei knew she had gone too far. What would she do? Where could she go? Steve returned from their bedroom and threw her clothes on the floor along with her suitcase. "Pack and leave!" he shouted at her.

Mei kneeled down and slowly folded each garment and placed it neatly in her suitcase. Steve stood over her watching and waiting. She could smell his booze and cigarettes. Mei walked to the door, put on her shoes and her coat, and dragging her suitcase behind her, she walked out of Steve Sutton's life and into a new life of her own making.

CHAPTER 37

As Poppy turned up Peninsula Road she saw a young Asian woman pulling a suitcase with difficulty on the gravel road. She was crying. It was a sad sight. The road was narrow and Poppy slowed down as she came to the girl in order to reduce the dust from billowing in her wake. The girl suddenly looked at her with instant recognition. Poppy had no idea who she was. She wound down the window and stopped beside her. "Can I help you? " she asked.

Mei was relieved to see the familiar car. She presumed this nice lady lived somewhere up Peninsula Road as she had seen her car coming downhill that day she had found the body. "I am hoping to find a ride to Auckland," she replied.

"It is over 3 miles to the main highway and it is getting late. You should stay somewhere locally tonight and take the trip tomorrow. There is a bus that leaves from Kaeo for Auckland but that is about thirty minutes away by car."

Poppy could tell the girl was in trouble. "Tell you what. I am staying at Tiromoana just up the road.

Hop in and we will see if there is a spare cabin for tonight."

"You mean at Audrey's place?" the girl asked.

"You know Audrey?" Poppy was surprised.

"Yes, I met her today. She is nice."

"Well, then, I am sure she will help you."

Mei got into Poppy's car and remained silent as they made their way up Peninsula Road to Tiromoana.

When Poppy explained Mei's situation to Audrey she was only too happy to open up a cabin for the night for Mei. "Tomorrow we will check on the bus schedule to Auckland. I can drop you at the bus stop in Kaeo. Get some sleep tonight and I'll see you in the morning." Audrey handed Mei some clean towels and bade her goodnight.

Poppy knew Audrey was responsible for her meeting with Detective Inspector Bromley. She had managed to cover her tracks and put suspicion upon Poppy. She was clever. And here she was acting all obliging and helpful. Had Audrey put her scarf at the scene? But when, how? Audrey could have easily gone into her cabin at anytime and removed her scarf. But why? Why would Audrey frame her? There could only be one reason. Audrey had something to hide. Poppy knew she needed to outsmart her. Tomorrow she would research some surveillance equipment. Audrey may have got away with murder this time. But Poppy wouldn't let that happen again. Tomorrow she would make a call. She would set up the perfect murder trap.

CHAPTER 38

Paul Riley turned the corner in his new Mercedes and sped onto the onramp of the Auckland motorway. He was late for his appointment with the head of Mission Finance, the biggest and most prestigious firm in offshore banking in the city. Paul had been with the firm for almost twenty years and realized his time had come for a major promotion. He had done good work over the years bringing in thousands of new clients and maintaining a steady flow of income for both he and the company.

Pulling into his personal parking space he reached for his briefcase and made his way inside the lobby of the glass and chrome high rise. They were waiting for him in conference room ten. He straightened his tie and checked the shine on his shoes. Paul was a meticulous dresser and knew today he wanted to look his best. As he opened the door all heads turned in his direction. Apologizing for his tardiness, Paul took the only empty seat at the table.

It took all of twenty minutes. Just twenty minutes, after twenty years of service, to tell him his skills were no longer required. A new, young team of financial geniuses would be assuming his position. He was offered a comfortable severance package if he would hand in his notice immediately.

He knew he had no choice. Fighting them would be costly and there was no assurance he would win. He accepted their offer, cleared out his desk, and departed the building. He looked at his phone, the meeting was at eight, it was nine thirty when he returned to his car and headed home. It took only one hour and thirty minutes to erase all trace of his existence at Mission Finance.

His north shore apartment was still mortgaged. He knew he couldn't afford the property taxes and monthly mortgage payments with his measly severance package. He had put his personal life on hold so he could build a career. Now he had no career and no personal life. Maybe he should have married, had a couple of kids and bought a nice bungalow down by the seaside at Mission bay. Instead he was single, unfit and had lost his youth along with his good looks at least ten years ago.

Pouring himself a stiff scotch he turned on CNN to watch the news, when his phone rang.

"Riley" he answered. It was his one and only friend outside work, Barney Dugger. "Barney, you old bugger, how are you? Nope doing nothing. You won't believe it. I got let go today at Mission. Can you believe it? Twenty years and I am being replaced by a bunch of bottle suckers! Would love to. When are you going? Count me in."

Paul poured another scotch and opened his laptop and ran a search: 'fishing in northland'. His mate was heading to Manganui with his boat for a week of fishing. He sat back and ran his hand through his thinning hair. The wide-open seas, big game fishing and beer – what more could a man want. Fuck Mission Finance! He was going fishing.

CHAPTER 39

Barney Dugger was looking forward to a week away fishing. Last night he got a call from his niece, Poppy.

"Uncle Barney, I really need your help. Do you think you could bring your boat and come up to Mangonui for a week or so?"

Barney's life was his own and he adored his niece. "Sure thing Poppy. Are you OK? Not in any trouble or anything?"

"Oh no. I am fine. I just need some help with a project I am working on. I need some advice and a little professional help."

Barney was an old-time investigator. Had been doing it for years. Mostly divorces and insurance frauds and, occasionally, work for the police. He wondered why Poppy would need his help.

"I'll leave this afternoon. Is it OK if I bring a buddy of mine? Helps to have two hands on board."

"That would be fine. Give me call when you arrive in Mangonui. Do you want to stay on the boat or onshore?"

"Maybe stay onshore a couple of nights. Where are you staying?"

"I am staying at Tiromoana Cabins at Hihi. I know they have vacancies at the moment. Do you want me to book you a couple of cabins?"

"Might as well. Then we can catch up and you can explain what you need. I will need to drop off the boat at Mangonui first."

"Great, I'll text you through the directions to Tiromoana. Call me when you get to Mangonui."

"Will do."

Barney couldn't imagine what was troubling his favorite niece. She was a pretty young thing. All hair and eyes. She looked just like her mother who had passed away when Poppy was just a teenager. Barney had taken on the role of parent ever since. Poppy's father wasn't in the picture and her brother had been found dead a few years ago. Suicide they said. Poppy never believed it was. He hoped she had moved on.

He heard his friend's car pull up in his driveway. Together they packed the boat and car and headed north.

CHAPTER 40

Audrey looked up as Poppy entered the office. "Hi Poppy, what's up?"

"Do you have a couple of cabins available for a couple of days. I just heard my uncle and his friend are coming up with their boat for a week of fishing and I suggested they stay here before they head off."

"Yes, I do. No problem." Audrey handed Poppy a registration form for her to fill in.

"I will put the cabins in my uncle's name, Barney Dugger." She wrote down his address and phone number. "I am not sure who is friend is. Will that do?"

"Yes, perfect. Do you want the keys, or will they check in with me first?"

"I'll take the keys. I will let him know I have them." Poppy took the keys and headed off into the sunshine.

Audrey noticed Poppy seemed to have an extra skip in her stride. She is up to something. I wonder what?

Mei entered the office looking like she hadn't had a wink of sleep. "I think I should go back to Steve. It is not his fault I don't like it there. If I leave my parents will be shamed. I am sorry Audrey. You have been so kind to me."

Audrey looked at the young girl. "Are you sure? Mei nodded. "Let me go over there with you. I just want to check you are OK."

"You would? That would be good." Mei reached for her suitcase and Audrey followed her out the door.

"We'll take the car. Saves pulling your suitcase up the driveways."

Steve Sutton looked furious when he opened the door to them. "Came running back," he smirked. "Who are you?"

"Pleased to meet you. I am your neighbor, Audrey Wetherby. Mei stayed with us last night. She just needed a little female company."

"So you are back to stay?" he asked Mei.

"Yes. I am sorry." Mei whispered with her head hung low.

"Well don't just stand there. Come in."

"I can't stay," said Audrey quickly. "I have guests checking in shortly. Bye Mei. Don't be a stranger. Pop on over when you feel like it."

Steve Sutton slammed the door. Audrey could hear him cursing Mei through the door as she left. That man needs to go. What a shit!

Returning to Tiromoana, Audrey stopped to talk to a trapper setting bait.

"Lots of activity up the road," he said.

"Have they removed all the wreckage?" Audrey asked.

"Yep. All gone. What the hell the guy was doing up there, I can't figure. Nothing up there. Drunk as a skunk they say. Still has a bad odor. Just set up new traps there."

Audrey hoped the whole matter was put to bed. Drunk driving was the latest update. She guessed Poppy had accepted she had nothing to do with it. So why was she looking so smug?

All this being so bloody neighborly was out of character for Audrey. She needed something to take her mind off things. The blue skies and endless sunshine wasn't helping.

CHAPTER 41

It was case closed. Bromley couldn't find any reason to keep the case open any longer. The man's toxicology report had confirmed he was extremely intoxicated at the time of the accident. There was no proof of foul play. Poppy's weak attempt at pointing the blame at Audrey Wetherby was nothing but an act of revenge for her brother's death Poppy had done nothing illegal. Her silk scarf must have simply been carried by a breeze and placed in the scene. Deep down the inspector was pleased he could put Poppy in the clear. It was an excuse to visit her and share the good news. He took a deep breath and felt the stress dissipating. He didn't need another crime taking place in his territory. He would visit Poppy at Tiromoana this afternoon. The thought excited him. Maybe he would wait until this evening. She might even invite him in for a drink. He would be off duty.

His phone rang. A domestic dispute in Hihi. A young girl has been badly beaten. Damn! He and his constable headed out of town with sirens blaring. Hihi was a ten-minute drive from his station. The report came in. It was a Chinese girl named Mei

Wong. He recognized the name as the girl who had found the body up the Peninsula. The address was next door to Audrey's. He knew it well.

They pulled up to the house and were met by the trapper who had made the call to 111. He had heard the screams and found the girl lying on the floor inside the front door. There was no sign of Steve Sutton, the owner of the house. The girl was bleeding badly. Her face was unrecognizable. Her small body was curled into a fetal position. The ambulance had just arrived. The men checked her pulse. It was weak. Bromley was saddened by the scene. Bloody old men bringing over young Asian brides. It sickened him. The poor girl. Photos were taken of the scene. The girl would survive. She was the only witness of the crime.

Steve Sutton had some serious explaining to do. He put an alert out to find the man. He drove a black range rover. He couldn't get far.

Domestic violence was taken seriously by the courts. New Zealand has the worse rate of family and intimate-partner violence in the world. A shocking 80 percent of incidents go unreported. One in three women experience physical and/or sexual violence in their lifetime. It costs the country between four and seven billion dollars a year. Bromley was familiar with the statistics with Northland being one of the most affected regions in the country. He knew it would be difficult to get Mei to press charges against Sutton. Even then, the man is likely to just get a few months in jail and a fine. Not enough in Bromley's book.

They took a statement from the trapper. He was visibly shaken by the incident. He said he was setting traps on the property when he heard her screams. When he got to the house, the door was wide open and there was no sign of Sutton. The girl was moaning but not responsive. She was still breathing and he immediately called 111. Sutton's car was not in the garage and he had not seen it leave the property. He must have left immediately before he got to the house. He thought he heard a car, but wasn't sure. It all happened so fast. Plus the trapper rode his quad bike to the house through the bush, which would have prevented him from hearing another vehicle. He confirmed only Sutton and the girl lived at the premises.

Bromley decided to stop off at Tiromoana next door and have a talk to Audrey and see if she had seen the girl or heard anything.

As he pulled up the driveway he saw Audrey talking to Poppy in the car park. They looked in his direction. Poppy immediately got into her car and headed past him down the drive. She looked like she was in a hurry. He was disappointed she didn't stay and talk to him. Obviously their last meeting had dampened their budding friendship.

CHAPTER 42

Well, there you are. He bloody did it! He beat her to a pulp. Audrey was livid! She had told Detective Inspector Bromley about Mei's decision to leave Steve Sutton the day before. How she had stayed in one of her cabins overnight and her decision to return to Steve that morning. Audrey had taken her home and heard Sutton yelling through the door when she left. If she had known what he was about to do she would never had left Mei there.

Now she had one thing on her mind - find Steve Sutton. Her afternoon was pretty free. All her guests were taken care of. She had time on her hands. She had seen Steve's range rover when she had dropped off Mei. She presumed he had escaped in it. Bromley said they had an alert out for him and asked Audrey to report any sightings of him.

Where would he go? He wouldn't take the main highways and risk being spotted. She wondered if he had simply driven down to one of his private beaches and taken his boat out. She saw it wasn't in the boat shed when she was there. Audrey noticed little details like that. She had spent a lifetime taking care of details. Murder was a skill and one she had perfected. She left her car in the car park and made her way on foot to the property next door. She took the bush track leading down to the water-front knowing it wasn't visible from the house. She presumed Sutton had taken the car to mislead the police. As she reached the middle of the track she could see the house in the distance. There was a police car parked out front and a couple of police guarding the property. They were waiting for Sutton to return, she guessed. Fat chance of that!

As she proceeded down the track, access was getting more and more difficult. Overgrown brush and gorse scraped at her arms as she pushed them aside. Finally she reached the shore. She would need to scramble over the rocky cliff face to reach the far beach, where she presumed Sutton had launched his boat. She was right. His car was hidden in the bush on the other side of the beach. She could see his boat still cruising in the shallow water and heading out to sea. Damn! She was too late! She sat on the shore and waited. The boat took a sharp turn to the right and disappeared into a cove further down the peninsula. I've got him.

Audrey continued around the shoreline keeping hidden by the overgrown bush bordering the shore. Finally she came to the boat moored just off shore and hidden in a small cove. There was no sign of Sutton. She spotted a small shed not far from the water's edge. This land was still on his property. She stayed hidden in the scrub and watched the shed for any sign of him. She was glad she had bought some supplies with her and opened a bag of almonds and waited.

She saw him. He was obviously drunk. He staggered into the shed holding a pile of firewood. She watched as a thin stream of smoke appeared from a small chimney on the old, shed roof. She realized that it was dusk. The nights can be cold. He was obviously planning on camping here until the morning.

This man needed to pay for what he had done. He didn't deserve Mei or this piece of paradise. Audrey reached for her supplies in her bag and made her way over to the shed. A bottle of scotch, GHB and an unfortunate boating accident would take care of everything. Mei would be free. She knocked at the old slatted door.

CHAPTER 43

P oppy was on a mission. She was heading west to Kaitaia to pick up surveillance equipment. Her Uncle may have brought some with him but she wanted to be sure she covered her bases. Technology today was amazing. She had found a distributor of the latest spy equipment including Wi-Fi smoke detector hidden cameras. They store up to eighty-six hours of video but take ten hours to charge. Tomorrow she would put one in each of their cabins and a couple in Audrey's cottage. She could hardly contain her excitement.

Poppy had left Tiromoana just as the Detective Inspector arrived. She had heard the sirens and guessed they were checking the old crash site. She didn't feel like talking to him. He had been almost rude accusing her of destroying evidence and taking Audrey's side of things. Well damn him! She would prove Audrey Wetherby was no sweet angel. Until then she would keep her distance. The news the man's death was caused by drunk driving and the police had closed the case, thankfully relieved her of any further involvement. She had the photos and would use them in her book anyway.

It was almost four pm when she arrived back at Tiromoana. Her Uncle had already moored his boat at Mangonui and was making his way back to the cabins to meet her. Audrey's car was parked in her usual spot. Poppy didn't have to wait long before her uncle arrived in his four-wheel drive with his empty boat trailer in tow. She was pleased to see him. He was her only real family now. He introduced her to his friend, Paul Riley. Poppy knew immediately he would make perfect bait. He was a dapper dresser, older man with rugged good looks. Tomorrow night she would arrange a get together with Audrey. A BBQ maybe if the weather permitted.

The men checked into their cabins and were pleasantly surprised with the rustic elegance of their surroundings. Hot tubs on their decks, full kitchens, fridges, ovens and even a complimentary bottle of wine welcomed them.

"Nice digs" Barney commented as he dropped his bags on the floor and put beer in the fridge. "Could rest my bones here awhile, no trouble."

Poppy smiled. It was nice to see her uncle again. She was happy just watching him making himself at home in the little cabin. She had already begun charging her collection of smoke alarm cameras. Tonight she would fill her uncle in on what she suspected. She knew he would help her. Poppy had made a tasty lamb chop casserole with mashed potatoes and local, home-grown, green beans. The men joined her for dinner and a hot tub. When Paul Riley retired to his cabin, Poppy and Uncle Barney stayed up talking until the wee hours of the morning.

CHAPTER 44

S he felt the barrel of the shotgun in the nape of her neck.
She had no doubt it was loaded.

"What the fuck are you doing here?" The man looked around in expectation. "Who else is here?"

"No-one. I am here alone. I was taking a walk along the shoreline and spotted your chimney fire. You know the cops are looking for you? Before you shoot me, I have something for you. Do you mind?" Audrey reached into her backpack and presented a bottle of scotch. "Thought you might need a drink, neighbor," she smiled her warmest smile.

"Well fuck me! Come on in. It must be my lucky night."

Audrey was surprised at how organized the little shed was. A bed in the corner, neatly made. A kitchen bench, wetback fireplace, small wood table and two chairs. The shed looked more spacious on the inside. She sat at the table while he grabbed a couple of glasses from a shelf on the far wall. He poured two glasses and took a large gulp. "I thought you were Mei's best friend?"

"Mei is lost. She is out of her comfort zone. It must be difficult leaving family and traveling to a strange country." Audrey figured the man had no idea he was being tracked by every policeman within the region.

"She pissed me off! Cost me a fortune to bring her over here. What more could she want? This is a multi-million-dollar property, anyone's dream. A great house, boat, beaches, bush – I just don't understand."

"You are right. You can offer her everything except the one thing she wants."

"What's that?"

"An education. She wants to study. She is young."

"She is a lousy lay," he said eyeing her with interest.

"What are you going to do now? There's a lot of commotion at your place. Police everywhere. You are a pretty popular guy."

"I have supplies. I can stay here or on my boat. Either way."

Audrey waited until the man went to stoke the fire, reached into her bag and quickly transferred a small pinch of GHB into his glass. "You hurt her very badly," she said.

"Fuck her! She got what she deserved."

Audrey watched as Steve continued to pour more whisky into his glass. As he stoked the fire, she continued to spike his glass. When she saw he was almost comatose she walked outside and called to him, "Steve, it looks as though your boat has come loose. Do you want me to tie it down again?"

The man left the shed and staggered towards the boat. As he pulled on the rope, he fell face first into the water. Audrey tied the rope around his waist and pushed his small boat out into the bay. It was a beautiful night. The stars were bright. She waited until the boat drifted out of sight. She returned to the shed, put out the fire, washed the glasses, wiped her fingerprints of the bottle of scotch, picked up her bag and closed the door. Audrey liked to leave things tidy. She hadn't realized how far around the bay she had walked. It took almost an hour to retrace her steps back to Tiromoana with just the light of her torch to guide her. The night air was filled with the sounds of moreporks, kiwis and pukekos. She could hear the waves lapping against the rocky shore. She felt good.

She had done this for Mei. Men like Steve Sutton didn't deserve to live. Arrogant, chauvinistic, mean, drunkard and abusive.

As she reached her cottage she heard laughter coming from the cabins on the ridge. Poppy's Uncle and his friend are having a nice time. Hopefully she is going to move on and let the past stay in the past.

Audrey had a clear conscience knowing she had nothing to do with her brother's death - that was her sister, Becka's doing, and she was on the other side of the world.

CHAPTER 45

Detective Inspector Bromley checked with Whangarei Hospital on Mei. They said she was doing as well as could be expected. She would survive. She had broken ribs, fractured cheekbone and multiple cuts and bruises. Bromley had seen many domestic violence cases but Mei's case was exceptionally brutal. Steve Sutton had only moved into the area a few months ago and after a background check, Bromley realized he had a history of domestic violence. He needed to be apprehended as quickly as possible.

The search area had widened to a national search. It had been almost twenty-four hours and Sutton could be anywhere. The airports had been notified. There had been no sightings of his range rover. The police wondered if he had gone to ground - hiding in the bush somewhere. Bromley organized a dog search on the Hihi peninsula. Sutton owned a large portion of the land and most of it was covered in native bush.

Bromley couldn't sit in his office any longer. He joined his team who were gathering at Sutton's house in preparation for the ground search. One of the constables asked, "Hey does

Sutton own a boat? There is a ton of boating gear here and no boat."

If the car and boat were missing there was a possibility Sutton had gone to sea. Bromley called the coastguard and requested a search of Doubtless Bay and surrounding areas. Maybe they could spot his range rover at a loading dock along the shoreline.

Unfortunately Bromley's team could not find any living relative of Steve Sutton. Researching his past they learned he had spent a number of years in the minefields of Australia then returned to New Zealand in the eighties and purchased a sheep farm in the Waikato region. No record of a wife or family. He was a solitary man, kept to himself. His criminal background dated back to his days in Australia. He had beaten a woman in a domestic dispute and done prison time over there.

He looked up as one of their helicopters circled above them. If Sutton was anywhere on the peninsula they had a good chance of finding him. If he had taken to sea, it would be more difficult.

It didn't take more than thirty minutes to hear the helicopter had spotted his range rover, partially hidden in bush near the shoreline, a few bays across from the house. A couple of minutes later there was another report of a boat drifting offshore a couple of miles further up shoreline. A shed or small hut was close to the site. It would appear the only access to the area was by sea. The hut and small coves were heavily covered in native bush. Access by road would be difficult.

The team joined the coastguard at Sutton's beach, near the house and followed the shoreline around to the designated locations. Two constables disembarked at the Range Rover location and the others went on to check out the boat and shed.

It didn't take long to realize Sutton was a dead man. The rope wound around his body had anchored his boat just fifty feet offshore. He had obviously been in the water for some time. Forensics later confirmed he had died between six and eight the night before.

Finding the remains of a recently lit fire in the nearby shed, an empty bottle of scotch and a half eaten can of baked beans indicated Sutton had been hiding out there prior to his death.

"Drunk himself stupid," a constable said as they returned to the station.

CHAPTER 46

Audrey had a secret. Well Audrey had lots of secrets but this was the mother of all secrets and definitely dangerous if it became known. She kept a record of each and every 'project' she had ever completed. She knew it would never be discovered. She was always careful.

She closed her curtains, locked the cottage doors, climbed the ladder to the mezzanine floor and removed a small silver box. The contents were benign – just a tiny LED projector and some black light pens. Returning to the lower level she plugged the projector into her computer and Googled the familiar map of Northland. Shining the map onto her ceiling, she moved the ladder so she could reach just the spot she wanted. Then, with her black light pen, she marked a tiny star on the ceiling. Each of her victims had a different colored star. Mr. Sutton's star was purple. Only Audrey knew the code. She lay on the floor looking at the ceiling. Every star carefully marked in its geographical location. This was Audrey's secret. She lay there for a long time tracing in her mind each and every project. Some were planned, others were unexpected – but all of them were justified.

Today she would stay in. Her cabins were all self-contained. The guests were responsible for their own meals. Later she would drop off fresh linens and see if they required the cabins to be serviced. Otherwise, she had the day to herself.

She heard the helicopter flying overhead. Earlier she had heard cars crunching up the long gravel driveway next door. She presumed they were searching for Steve Sutton. She looked at his star on the ceiling and smiled. They would find him soon. It would look like a drunken attempt to escape in his boat. She hoped Mei was OK. What a bastard he was.

Domestic violence cases rarely make the news. They are too common. Finding Sutton's body trapped in his boat's anchor rope would probably make the evening news. Especially as it involved a police search. Audrey knew Sutton would have only received a small, if any, prison sentence and a minimum fine for beating poor Mei to a pulp. She felt vindicated in sentencing him to death.

Her phone rang, she let it go to voicemail.

Whatever it was, it could wait.

CHAPTER 47

Poppy awoke excited and motivated for a day of investigation. Her Uncle Barney had agreed to assist with the placing of the smoke detector cameras. They were identical in design to the ones Audrey had in the cabins. Her plan was to replace the ones in their cabins first and test them. As soon as Audrey left her cottage they would replace hers.

Uncle Barney was a little skeptical at first when Poppy shared her suspicions about Audrey's responsibility for multiple murders in the area, but he loved his niece and if it made her happy, he would help her.

They worked! Poppy watched on her computer while her Uncle obligingly paced up and down in his cabin. She had no doubt Audrey could be enticed into spying on her again. Now she just had to wait until Audrey left her cottage.

Poppy's second plan was to set up Uncle Barney's friend, Paul Riley, as bait for Audrey. She made her way over to Audrey's cottage to invite Audrey to a BBQ tonight. She was disappointed to see no-one was at the office and the cottage curtains were closed. She must be having a day off. She reached for her cell phone and called Audrey's number. No answer. She left a message. Her car was still in the car park. Maybe she was walking the property. She returned to the men and they all agreed to take the boat out for spin. They would be back in plenty of time for dinner.

Once their boat was heading out into Doubtless Bay they saw the coastguard and a police boat over by the Hihi peninsula.

"Let's go and see what all the fuss is about," Poppy said excitedly pointing in the direction of the commotion.

"I heard a helicopter earlier flying overhead. They must have found someone or something," said Paul.

"There were a lot of cars coming and going up the road this morning. I wondered what the fuss was about?"

Poppy was annoyed she had missed out on the action and checked her phone for a news update. "Here it is!" she said. "A man's body has been found in Doubtless Bay. Police are on the scene. Shit! I wonder who it is? "

As their boat approached the area the police waved them away. It was obvious they couldn't get any closer.

"Damn!" said Poppy. She called Detective Inspector Bromley and just got his voicemail. She didn't leave a message. Her curiosity was killing her. The men took the boat out further towards the open sea and they spent the next few hours drinking beers and fishing. The day was warm, sunny and breezy. By four o'clock they had caught enough fish for a first-class BBQ and made their way back to the dock.

All afternoon, Poppy was checking her phone. There were no updates relating to the body. Hopefully it would be on tonight's news.

They were back at Tiromoana by five thirty. Poppy had stopped at the Four Square supermarket in Mangonui to pick up supplies for dinner. She knew Audrey liked a good Sauvignon

Blanc. Dropping off the supplies at her cabin she headed over to Audrey's cottage. She knocked at her door. No reply. She called her cell. No reply. She left another message "Audrey, Poppy here. We've been out fishing and are planning a BBQ this evening. We would love you to join us. Call me."

All she could do was wait for her to reply.

CHAPTER 48

Audrey was tucked up in bed watching movies. She had serviced all the cabins, dropped off fresh linens and provided a complimentary bottle of wine in each fridge. She hoped that would allow her to be left alone tonight. She was tired. She always experienced a real high after she had completed a project, followed by a feeling of utter exhaustion. She had heard the news they had found a body on the waterfront nearby.

She saw she had a message on her phone. She listened. Oh No! The last thing she wanted to do was to socialize with her guests. Audrey was an introvert ninety percent of the time. She could be lively, entertaining and even likeable but that was definitely limited to specific social necessities. Having a meal with guests was not on her list of 'musts'. She returned a quick text, *Sorry unable to join you for dinner.* Short and the point. She checked the time it was seven o'clock. She hoped they hadn't waited for her. Oh well. She thought it strange Poppy suddenly wanted to be her friend after accusing her of killing her brother.

Or did Poppy have other plans? Audrey sensed she needed to be careful. Poppy was up to something.

While she had her movie on pause, she decided to call Whangarei Hospital and check on Mei. She was surprised when the ward nurse offered to put Mei on the phone. She sounded tired and frightened. "Have you spoken to your parents?" asked Audrey.

"No. I don't want them to know about this," she said.

"Have you heard about Steve?" Audrey asked.

"The police talked to me this afternoon. They told me they found him dead in the water."

"Did they say how he died?"

"They said it was an accident. He got tied up in a rope or something trying to get into his boat. I didn't understand exactly what they were saying. Oh Audrey, I don't know what to do now. I can't go back to the house and I can't go home."

"Mei, of course you can go back to the house. You were his fiancé. When are they going to discharge you?"

"They said I could go home in a couple of days."

"Would you like me to pick you up? "

"I don't want to bother you. You have been so

kind to me. But maybe I could stay at Steve's house until I am well enough to move to Auckland. I still want to do my studies."

Audrey gave Mei her number and agreed to drive her back to Hihi when she was discharged. It was the least she could do.

Audrey pushed 'play,' laid back on her pillows and continued watching "The Talented Mr. Ripley" - her favorite movie of all time.

CHAPTER 49

D etective Inspector Bromley returned from his interview with the press. Domestic violence was something he couldn't tolerate. In his interview he had made a point of condemning the dead man.

He stated, "Mr. Steve Sutton was wanted by the police for a serious domestic violence incident. He chose to evade the police and in his attempt to flee the scene, he caused his own demise. His body was found in a rocky cove adjoining his own property on the Hihi Peninsula. His death has been confirmed as an accident and the police are not pursuing anyone else in relation to the incident."

Bromley had called again to check on Mei's condition and was informed she would be released in a couple of days. He was pleased. He hoped she was in contact with her parents and would be returning to China. It had not been a good choice to accept Steve Sutton's hospitality, if you could call it that.

He saw Poppy had called his cell phone earlier that day. She had not left a message. He checked the time. It was still early. He returned her call.

"Inspector Bromley, thank you for getting back to me. I was out in my uncle's boat this afternoon and saw all the commotion by the Hihi Peninsula. I realize now, after hearing the news, it was Mei's fiancé whose body you found. How is Mei? Is she all right?"

"Mei is at the Whangarei Hospital. She is improving but will be sore for some time. She was hurt rather badly."

"So the man drowned in the bay was caught in a rope, I heard."

"Yes, drunk and careless."

"I just can't believe it. Two accidents in the same week and both on the Hihi peninsula."

"Leave it alone, Poppy. I know what you are thinking. Accidents happen."

Poppy laughed. "You know me well enough. At least my scarf wasn't found tied to the boat."

"Just as well," Bromley chuckled.

"Well, thanks for getting back to me."

"You're welcome," Bromley ended the call and wondered why Poppy had really called him. He told her nothing the television reporters hadn't already informed the public. It had been all over the news. He wondered what she was up to. Trouble no doubt.

He was looking forward to an early night. His wife had gone for a few days to visit her sister. He was alone. His thoughts went to Poppy. He wished he had been brave enough to ask her out to dinner on some pretense. Unfortunately he wasn't a natural philanderer. Maybe just as well.

CHAPTER 50

Audrey couldn't resist. She set up the ceiling map and lay on a cushion on the floor. In the dark the iridescent stars shone brightly like stars revealing the exact location of each body, each murder, each project. She never kept the map on her computer and always deleted her search history afterwards. Without the map the ceiling stars looked random in design. In the daylight they were invisible to the naked eye. Audrey recreated the murder map whenever she moved to a new location. Over the years the number of stars grew and the locations widened. Hihi was lit up like the fourth of July. It was her secret world – a world only she knew existed.

Never being able to share your achievements made her life seem unimportant. Lonely even. She had come to learn one of her sister's shared her love of murder but they had never confided in each other. Best left unsaid, unspoken. One day, maybe. She turned off the projector, deleted the map and poured another glass of wine. She could hear Poppy and her friends in the distance. They appeared to be having quite a party.

She turned off her bedside light and fell into a dreamless sleep.

It was almost noon before Audrey awoke to face the day. She felt revived, fresh, happy even. She picked up the large cushion from the floor – a reminder of her late night habit, and took a long soak in the bath. She didn't have any guests checking out today. It was a perfect spring day to attack the weeds in the garden. Every year she barked her gardens to keep weeds to a minimum. Native pungas, ferns, flaxes, fruit trees, and succulents adorned her gardens and created natural borders for her lawns and pathways. She donned her gardening hat and gloves, filled her wheelbarrow with rakes, spades, clippers, forks and a hoe and set off to spend the day with nature.

She saw him silhouetted against the midday sun. His voice deep and enticing "Hello. Beautiful gardens you have here. They must keep you busy?"

Audrey held her hand over her eyes to shade out the glare. "Thank you. Are you a gardener too?"

"Haven't really had the time until recently. But yes, I do like to garden. When I was a boy, I had the biggest and best vegetable garden in our street." He laughed.

"I have a small vegetable garden but it is difficult in the summertime with the water shortage. I only have rainwater storage here at Tiromoana. Three tanks are not quite enough to keep a vegetable garden alive during the dry months." Audrey realized she was babbling on.

"How long have you owned this place?" the man asked as he bent down beside her giving Audrey a more accurate view of a man she could easily fall in love with. He was tall, immaculately dressed and smelled divine.

"A few years now. It was only a cottage and one cabin when I purchase it. I have since added the other cabins." She realized she had no idea to whom she was talking. "I'm sorry, but we haven't met. I am Audrey Wetherby. You must be Poppy's friend."

"Paul Riley. Nice to meet you, Audrey Wetherby."

"How is your cabin? Everything all right?"

"Yes, very comfortable. It was a shame you couldn't join us last night for dinner."

"I am sorry. I was exhausted. I had a busy day and with all the commotion going on with my neighbors next door, I just wanted an early night." Audrey smiled her prettiest smile.

"How about tonight? Tomorrow Barney and I are taking the boat out for a few days. At least join us for a drink," he pressed.

"I'll see how my day goes. But, thanks. That is very kind of you."

Audrey realized her heart was beating faster and her breaths were becoming shorter and shorter. She felt flushed. Damn! He is gorgeous! Why did good-looking men always make her nervous? It wasn't until she returned inside for a glass of cold water did she realize her face was covered in mud, her hair contained chunks of god knows what and foreign nasty things clung to her berry stained top. Great!

CHAPTER 51

M ei was worried about returning to Steve's house. She knew he had no relatives. They had discussed it many times. Mei was surprised. Family was an important part of Mei's life. She wondered who would inherit the house. Mei wasn't stupid, she wondered if she might be able to claim the inheritance as his fiancé. A quick check online clearly indicated she could only qualify if she had been living with him in a de facto relationship for at least three years. Then she read; if the relationship was for less than three years, the de facto partner has no right to receive under the intestacy rules, unless the court is satisfied *there is a child of the relationship.*

A child! Mei realized she could be pregnant. The man had raped her the first night she arrived. He had continued to have sex with her until that fateful day when he attacked her. Could she be pregnant? She wondered if the nightmare she had been living could turn out to be her good fortune. Another online search advised only a blood test could confirm pregnancy only five days since conception. She rang the bell for the nurse.

"I am worried I am pregnant. Do you think you could

arrange a blood test? I forgot to ask the doctor. Can you tell after only five days?"

The nurse looked at Mei with sympathy. "You poor dear. You have been through so much. I will ask the doctor. I'll be back."

Mei felt alive for the first time since she had laid eyes on Steve Sutton. If she was pregnant, she could claim ownership of his estate. She would be a wealthy woman. Her life would change completely. She couldn't sleep, couldn't eat the anticipation was killing her. Finally, the nurse returned.

"The doctor said it is very early based on the dates in question and the result may not be 100% accurate. But he has agreed." She prepared the syringe, disinfected the area and withdrew the blood while Mei watched and prayed silently.

"How long before I get the results?"

"We have a lab here. It shouldn't take too long. But you should really have another test in a couple of weeks to confirm the results."

Mei nodded. "Thank you. You have been so kind."

The nurse left holding Mei's fate in her hands. If it were positive, the nightmare of the past week would have been worth it. She could breathe. All the pain she felt validated her right to Steve's fortune. His death had given her life. If only....

CHAPTER 52

The telephone rang as Audrey was running her bath. A glass of Sauvignon Blanc was sitting pretty on a shelf. The smell of eucalyptus oil penetrated the evening air. Wrapped in a large fluffy towel she answered the phone. It was Paul.

"Audrey we are just about to enjoy your sunset over a glass of wine, and I was hoping you would join us."

"I am just about to climb into a bath." She confessed.

"Should I come over there?" he teased.

She laughed. "I'll join you in about half an hour."

"See you soon."

Audrey's day in the sun provided a nice golden glow to her skin. She washed her hair and enjoyed the luxury of a deep bath while the tanks were still full.

Before she left she checked her reflection in the full-length mirror. She looked good. She had chosen a pale green wrap maxi dress with her favorite strappy sandals. Her new slender body and short blonde bob were the results of eating healthy and the talents of the local Taipa hairdresser. Audrey never went anywhere empty handed. Two bottles of Sauvignon Blanc and a plate of cold cooked shrimp would be welcome accompaniments she hoped.

She had forgotten how lovely the cabins looked at night. Poppy had put fairy lights on the deck. Each cabin had their own BBQ. Steve was turning over fillets of fish. He looked fabulous, dressed in jeans and a light blue sweater. Audrey joined Poppy and her uncle at the outside table placing the wine and shrimp next to bowls of salad and potato. Poppy introduced her to Uncle Barney – an older man who had obviously lived a rugged, hard life - quite the opposite from his friend, Paul, the dapper dresser and conservationist.

Audrey found she was enjoying herself. Paul was very attentive – refilling her empty glass, feeding her little "you've gotta taste this" bites and listening avidly to every story she told.

Audrey realized Poppy had disappeared. "Have you seen Poppy?" she asked.

"Barney and Poppy have gone for a walk to see if they can spot any kiwi birds," Paul said looking out into the darkness.

"I never even saw them leave." Audrey felt embarrassed. "Did you want to go too?"

"Oh no. I would much rather sit here and chat with you."

Audrey was flattered. "You are such a sweet talker" she joked. "I must be going. It is getting late. Tell Poppy and Barney I had a lovely time. Thank you for inviting me." She stood to leave.

Then she saw it. It was just a flicker of fear in his eyes. "Please stay a little longer. It is only early yet."

Audrey's heart sank. Where was Poppy? What was she up to? "Sorry Paul. Have a wonderful fishing trip. I really have to go."

She almost ran back to the cottage. As she reached the track to her back door she thought she saw a faint light moving in the cottage. She reached down to where she kept a key and unlocked the door. The cottage was empty. She pulled back the curtains and peered into the night. Two shadowy figures disappeared onto the ridge.

Suddenly it all made sense. She had been enticed away from her cottage so they could search it. But why? What were they looking for? Audrey didn't have anything of real value. Her computer was only used for business. She never kept a history of her searches. She decided to follow them back to their cabin and listen in on their conversation. She took a track through the bush and listened as they returned.

"Shit Paul, What happened. I thought she was all into you. Couldn't you stop her? She nearly caught us red handed."

"I tried. She just got up and left. Said she had to get back."

Poppy looked at the table. "She didn't even take her plate back. Did she notice we had gone somewhere?"

"I said you were looking for kiwis."

Audrey recognized Barney's voice. "At least we got them up. Hopefully they are working OK."

"Let's see." Poppy followed the men inside her cabin.

Audrey crept to the side window of the cabin. She was grateful for the moonless night. She watched as Poppy opened up her laptop and Audrey almost gasped as she saw her kitchen and living room appear on the screen. Another shot showed her bedroom. The cameras appeared to be high on the walls or ceiling. She felt violated. How dare they? Privacy was precious to Audrey. She returned to her cottage. It didn't take long to find the phony smoke alarms. She knew they were breaking the law. Unauthorized entry was illegal and invasion of privacy was actionable. She would go to bed tonight and act as though they weren't there. Tomorrow she would decide what to do. If only they knew they were playing a game they could never win.

CHAPTER 53

Mei's nurse came to tell her the sad news. "I am so sorry but the initial tests show the HCG hormone in your blood indicates there is a good chance you are pregnant. I am so sorry."

Mei asked. "Are you sure? I am pregnant?"

"You should have another test in a few weeks to confirm the results. But, yes, it looks as though you are. Are you sure you still want to go home today? Maybe you should stay another night?"

"No. I am fine. I will call my friend, Audrey. She said she would pick me up today. She lives about two hours away. So is it OK if I leave about noon?"

"Yes, that's fine. I will tell them to bring in your breakfast."

Mei texted Audrey to ask her to pick her up at noon and smiled. She may only be twenty-two years old, but she had outsmarted Mr. Steve Sutton. She was young, pregnant and rich. Things could be worse.

Mei was happy to see Audrey who looked quite taken back by her appearance. Mei was aware she looked pretty beat up. Her face was still swollen and her ribs were painful when she moved.

A nurse wheeled her out to Audrey's car and helped her into the passenger seat.

"I don't suppose you know an estate lawyer?" she asked.

"No, can't say I do. Why do you ask?"

"I have been doing some research while I was in the hospital. I have learned I might have a legal claim on Steve's property."

"Oh my God! How?" Audrey was intrigued.

"Steve told me he had no family, no living relatives and no ex-wives. He was engaged once to another Asian girl, but it didn't work out. A de facto partner has to have lived with the deceased for at least three years unless, she is pregnant."

"Well, that counts you out. You were living with him less than a week."

"I did a blood test while I was in hospital. I am pregnant."

"Oh Mei. Oh wow." Audrey laughed. "Serves the old bastard right. This is hilarious. You could own everything, his house, his property, his car, his boat, everything! Oh Mei." Audrey couldn't stop laughing.

"I am so sorry that you are pregnant but isn't fate a wonderful thing?"

Just talking about it made it seem possible to Mei. "I guess it is worth finding out if I have a claim."

"Absolutely. When we get back, we can find you a good estate lawyer. I guess I am taking you to your new home. Congratulations Mei. You are a clever girl!"

CHAPTER 54

When Audrey left Mei, she was settled into her new home next door. Good things happen to good people Audrey thought as she drove up her driveway. They had stopped for groceries on the way home and it was almost three o'clock.

She admired her gardens as she walked down the path towards the cottage. Spring flowers were in bloom.

Upon awaking that morning, Audrey had made a decision regarding the smoke alarms. Before heading to the hospital she had picked up twenty-one new smoke alarms from the Coopers Beach Hammer hardware and began to replace all the smoke alarms throughout the property. She started first with the guy's cabins. They had already left for a day of fishing. Each cabin had three alarms. Audrey took Poppy's alarms and placed them in a trash bag. She could see Poppy looking out her window as she made her way to the other three cabins armed with a large box of newly purchased smoke alarms. Before making her way over to Poppy's cabin she replaced all the smoke alarms in her office and cottage.

Knocking at the last cabin she was greeted by a nervous Poppy.

"Audrey," was all she could say.

"Hi Poppy, it is that time of year again. Our local fire service is a stickler for making sure we check all smoke alarms monthly. This year they are due for a replacement. She handed her a fire safety brochure. Do you mind? It will only take a few moments. Audrey made her way inside the cabin and climbed on one of the wooden chairs to reach the alarms. Poppy watched in horror as Audrey quickly removed Poppy's alarms and threw them into a bright yellow trash bag immediately installing new ones in their place. With a smile and a cheery "goodbye" Audrey threw the yellow trash bag over her shoulder and departed.

What could Poppy say? Leave them alone they are mine! Yeah right. She was trapped. As soon as Audrey returned to her cottage she removed the memory cards from Poppy's alarms and began to watch her guests' movements over the past twenty-four hours. Audrey wasn't a voyeur. After two minutes she was bored. Watching the personal habits of other people didn't excite her in the least. A quick check of the photos revealed nothing she didn't already know. She figured the cameras were installed in their cabins to film her snooping. Audrey was more interested in the memory cards from her cabin and office. Especially when she saw Poppy looking through her office files, checking her computer and going through her drawers. Poppy even had the audacity to go through Poppy's wardrobe, dresser drawers and personal items. Obviously taking advantage of her early visit to the hardware store.

When Audrey left to pick up Mei she collected all the recycling bins and cans, along with the trash bag full of alarms, with her. If Poppy went snooping trying to find the memory cards, she was out of luck.

Back in her office there was a message on her phone. "Audrey, Paul Riley here. Just wanted to say I really enjoyed your company last night. Barney and I are coming back to Tiromoana this evening – hope our cabins are still available. Decided it's a lot more comfortable sleeping there than on the boat. We are planning on eating at the Indian curry restaurant on the Mangonui Waterfront. Would love you to join us. See you about seven."

Bastard! Shithead! So suave, so good-looking and so bloody deceitful. But tempting, all the same.

Another voice message from the postman advised there was a parcel for her at the Mangonui post office.

She parked her car by the little restaurant on the corner and was surprised to see Poppy and Detective Inspector Bromley sitting at a corner table. She sat in her car and watched the pair. Poppy was flirting, flicking her hair, laughing and leaning close to the Inspector as she whispered something in his ear. He was absorbed, infatuated and obviously flattered by the beautiful woman's undivided attention. *So, Poppy and the Inspector are an item.* Is the inspector also involved in Poppy's covert pursuit of justice? Shit!

This made everything a lot more complicated. It was time for Poppy to find accommodation elsewhere. Tomorrow she would make some excuse to close down Tiromoana temporarily. She needed a little holiday anyway. Maintenance work, maybe. Poppy would have to find somewhere else to write her bloody true crime novel featuring, non-other, than herself.

Audrey pulled out of the car park. Parcel forgotten. She was livid! Fuck them both!

CHAPTER 55

Detective Inspector Bromley was surprised when Poppy suggested lunch in the village. He thought he had fucked up any chance of them being friends. Of course, a woman like that was never *just* a friend. If his wife saw him lunching with such a beautiful woman, he would be dead. Bromley knew he wanted more. His wife would not be back until the end of the week.

Poppy seemed to have only one thing on her mind. Proving Audrey was a killer. She seemed a little out of sorts. Troubled. He asked her how her book was progressing. Poppy said she was in the research stage and was working on a new development she couldn't talk about. She asked Bromley again if she could interview his daughter about her friend's murder. He flatly refused. The last thing he needed was to have his family involved again in the case. "The case is solved and closed," he told her. She pouted and sulked so beautifully he almost relented, but didn't.

Bromley hinted about meeting later for dinner. Poppy had plans with her uncle. "Another night then," he suggested. *Damn!* She was so bloody sexy. He wondered what her main purpose for asking him to lunch was. To tease? To feel wanted? For information? He couldn't be certain. When he arrived back at the station she texted him. *Dinner tomorrow night?* Damn! He was a lucky guy.

Bromley called Whangarei Hospital to check on Mei. He was told she had been discharged. A lady had picked her up. He asked whom and was told Audrey Wetherby. He wondered why Poppy believed Audrey was capable of multiple murders. This woman was kind and considerate. He phoned Audrey and got her answerphone. "Audrey, Detective Inspector Bromley. Just checking on Mei. I understand you picked her up from the hospital. Let me know how she is. Would appreciate it. Thanks."

He looked at Steve Sutton's file still sitting on his desk. The photos of Mei at the scene were horrendous. He wondered when she would be returning to China. He called the constable and told him to box up Suttons files and reports and mark them all "case closed."

CHAPTER 56

P oppy returned from her afternoon tea on the waterfront with Detective Inspector Bromley. It hadn't gone to plan. Nothing she could say would convince him of Audrey's guilt. Why? She wondered. What did Audrey have over him? Now she had to deal with the removal of all her spy cameras. Audrey knew of course. Why else would she suddenly replace all the smoke alarms? Audrey was on to her. Damn! They had cost a pretty penny and now were somewhere in the trash. When she thought of Audrey looking through the photos on the memory cards, she felt sick. She had obviously been caught in the act of going through her things. What a mess! Why had Audrey not reported her? Obviously, Audrey wanted to keep Poppy's unlawful entry into her home as evidence against her.

Uncle Barney and Paul arrived back from a day on the boat with a bucket load of fresh, filleted fish. Poppy put it in the freezer and they went their separate ways, to bathe and get dressed for dinner. When it was time to leave, Poppy couldn't find Paul anywhere. She called his cell and there was no reply. She checked his cabin once more and found it empty. Maybe he was with Audrey? She walked over to the office and found it closed for the night. She knocked at Audrey's door and got no reply. The cottage was in darkness. Maybe Paul had already left for the restaurant? Poppy and her uncle tried calling Paul again. They left a message to say they were leaving for the restaurant and would meet him there.

By the time Poppy arrived, the restaurant was packed. She had made reservations earlier in the day and they were ushered to a table by the window overlooking the bay. Ordering drinks they waited for Paul to join them. He never did. They ordered without him and spent the night discussing Audrey's latest move to replace all smoke alarms in an obvious message to Poppy that Audrey was on to her. Uncle Barney suggested he do some digging into the old police files relating to the cases Penny was researching. "I have some friends at the Whangarei and Kaeo police stations that might be able to help you," he offered. "When I get back home, I will give them a call and see if they will talk to you. A couple of them recently retired from the force and may be more willing to give you what you are looking for."

"You are a sweetheart, Uncle Barney. What would I do without you?"

Poppy looked at the time. It was eleven thirty and still no message from Paul. "Should we be worried, Uncle Barney?"

"No, he's a big boy. He can look after himself."

CHAPTER 57

Audrey was in no mood for company. Tomorrow she would shut down the cabins for a week feigning maintenance and repairs. When her guests left for dinner she would take over a "Closed for urgent maintenance" notice and pin it to their front door. Seeing Poppy cozying up to Detective Inspector Bromley was just taking it too far. She had formed a good relationship with the detective and Poppy's constant interference was really pissing her off.

Audrey sat at her computer printing off the signs and listening to the evening news. Steve Sutton's death was not even mentioned, it was already old news. She wondered how Mei was getting on next door. It still made her laugh to think of Mei inheriting all of Steve's money. A quick search for estate lawyers revealed a comprehensive list of companies in Kerikeri and beyond. She knew Mei would need to find out if there was a will involved and if so, who were the beneficiaries. If he had no family he may not have even written a will. She called Mei and gave her a couple of lawyer's names and suggested she call them tomorrow to start the process of claiming her rights to his inheritance. Mei sounded a little intimidated by everything but promised the make the calls. She said she was fine but tired.

It was nearing seven when she saw him standing at the glass sliding doors. Damn! She had not replied to his invite. Dinner with Poppy and her merry band of snoops was the last thing she needed right now. She had no choice. He had seen her. She opened the door and smiled pleasantly. "Paul Riley, what a surprise."

"Audrey Wetherby, you didn't reply to my invitation so I am here to escort you to dinner and I don't want a 'no.'"

"I am so sorry I should have replied. I have had an awful day and really just want a quiet night at home. Send my apologies to Poppy and Barney." Audrey's hand went to close the door.

"Wait. If you don't feel like being sociable, I understand. Why don't we just enjoy the evening and take a bottle of wine down to the beach and watch the sunset."

The bloody man looked so gorgeous and desirable, Audrey seriously considered his offer. "It is tempting I have to say. But really, I just feel like being alone this evening and I have some work I have to catch up on."

He wouldn't take no for an answer. "And miss an opportunity for the best Sauvignon Blanc you will ever taste in your life. I bought it especially for you. Look!" He exposed a bottle he was hiding behind his back and grinned like a schoolboy.

Audrey couldn't refuse. How could she? "OK just a quick drink and then I must get back to work."

"We had better head off down the track before the others come looking for us." He grinned.

"So we are playing hooky?"

"Yep. We are." He took Audrey by the arm and led her down the bush track towards Honeymoon Beach. It was a precarious climb down the clay steps covered in seasonal pine needles causing a slippery surface. Paul gallantly held her hand as they descended towards the overgrown track below. The sound of lapping water on the rocky beach was enticing. The evening was unseasonably warm. The sun was falling lower in the sky as they finally made their way to a large rock at the water's edge.

Paul produced a couple of wine glasses out of his pockets, which made Audrey laugh. "Always prepared I see."

Paul raised his glass, "To good wine and good company." He toasted.

"To good wine," she repeated.

CHAPTER 58

Mei couldn't believe it was only a week since she had arrived at Auckland airport and met Steve in person for the first time. It seemed deathly quiet in his big empty house. The phone never rang. She could hear her slippered feet pattering on the tiled floors as she walked from room to room. Steve had obviously been a bachelor. The décor was cold and stark - light gray walls, white tiles, chrome and glass furniture and floor to ceiling windows. The views across the bay and out to sea were breathtaking. Mei sat outside on the deck and watched the tuis dart among the teatrees. The nearest beach was visible from the house. She had gone to the beach with Steve the first day they arrived. Expansive mowed lawns circled the house and spread to the water's edge. She wondered who would mow the lawns now. She had seen the big ride-on mower parked in his open shed along with his quad bike, and boating gear. She didn't even know how to drive a car let alone operate all his vehicles.

The police had returned Steve's car and boat to the shed. Mei always rode a scooter at home and knew she would need to learn how to drive if she was to survive here. She would ask Audrey how to go about getting lessons.

She realized there was so much she didn't know. How would she pay the bills for the telephone, electricity and other household bills? Did Steve pay them automatically out of his bank account? Could she access his bank account? She knew she had to take control of things and walked back inside to the kitchen where she had left the names of the lawyers Audrey had kindly given her.

By lunchtime, Mei was in a clearer state of mind. She had found a wonderful lawyer, Guy Morris, of Morris, Main and Company. He was sympathetic and obliging. When he said he would be able to meet with her at four o'clock that afternoon, Mei explained her driving dilemma and he was kind enough to offer to drive all the way to Hihi to visit with her at the house. Just knowing she had someone who could advise her made her feel a thousand times better.

When Mei opened the door to greet her new lawyer, she was pleasantly surprised. He was Chinese. He explained he had been in New Zealand since high school and spoke both Mandarin and English. His English was much better than hers so they conversed in Mandarin. He was impressed with the research Mei had done concerning her possible rights to Steve Sutton's estate. He had already done a search and advised Mei Mr. Sutton had indeed not written a will. As there were no known relatives of Mr. Sutton, she was correct in assuming the property and assets would go to the Crown unless she could make a claim based on her status as his de facto partner who is pregnant with the deceased child.

Mei explained she had a pregnancy test done at the hospital but she would need to have another one in a couple of weeks to confirm it. Her lawyer agreed. "We have a lot of work to do in the meantime," he said. "First we have to apply for you to be appointed administrator of the estate."

Mei was impressed and grateful. Her new lawyer was not only extremely efficient he was quite cute. Mei found herself feeling comfortable for the first time since leaving her home in China. She could see Mr. Morris was not wearing a wedding ring. She wondered if he was a single man. She wished her face wasn't red and swollen. She had explained on the phone she was badly abused by her fiancé prior to his death. Mr. Morris was aware of the case along with most New Zealanders who watched the evening news.

Mei explained her monetary situation and her inability to pay him as Steve had been supporting her financially and there was only a small amount of cash in the house. He said he would find a way to get her access to some funds, at least initially, as they did have a verbal agreement. Mei agreed to forward him emails confirming Mr. Sutton's intention and agreement of Mia's financial support and imminent marriage.

Mei had been impressed when Mr. Morris removed his shoes upon entering the house. She waited while he donned his shoes as he was leaving. He reached into his wallet and withdrew two one hundred dollar bills. "Mei you need some money to buy groceries until I can get you access to some funds. I won't take no." He handed her the notes and she was humbled by his kindness.

"Thank you, Mr. Morris. I am so pleased to have met you."

"Don't you worry, I will call you tomorrow after I've got my head around all of this. In the meantime you just rest."

Mei watched him drive away in his Audi convertible. She closed the door and made her way to the black leather sofa by the fireplace. It was time to call her parents. It was not going to be easy.

CHAPTER 59

D avid Williams recognized the man's face in the paper from the old, framed photo on his Mother's dresser. When he asked if the man in the photo was his father, she refused to talk about it. It wasn't until his mother death last year when he found her letters addressed to Steve Sutton and marked "Return to Sender. Address Unknown" he suspected he was right.

Dear Steve,
You haven't written for so long I
wonder if you have forgotten me and the
wonderful time we spent together.
I really need to talk to you but when I
call the phone number you gave me it
says it is no longer in service.
I am hoping this letter finds you safe
and well.
You left without saying goodbye. I
awoke to find your note by my bedside.

You said you would call me and I have
been waiting by the phone.
Please, call me and let me know you are
all right.
I have something very important to
tell you.
Love Always
Naomi

It was sadly pathetic to know his mother has suffered all those years waiting in vane for a lover who never cared shit about her. It explained a lot about his childhood. She was a bitter woman who never married and died a sorry spinster. She had made his life hell.

It was the featured story in his local paper. The story of the man whose body was found floating in Hihi bay attached to an anchor rope that confirmed his suspicions. The article included photos of Steve Sutton's earlier mining and farming careers. David, having just turned forty-three, figured his father was only twenty years old when he was born and when he left his mother pregnant and alone. At least they had one thing in common. They both had anger issues. He read how his father had brutally beaten his fiancé and immediately fled the scene. What they didn't have in common was wealth. His father appeared to own a property up north near Mangonui. David owned a motorbike, a full body of tattoos and a membership in the Head Hunters motorcycle gang. His sole income derived from meth-amphetamine distribution provided a tidy income but nowhere near what his dead father has obviously accumulated during his life.

He read his father's fiancé was a mail-order bride from China who had just arrived a week prior to the incident. David saw his opportunity to cash in on his absentee father's death. The bastard didn't provide a penny for him or his mother when he was alive, now he was dead he was going to take what was owed to him.

David packed his bag, closed the door on his sorry life, mounted his Harley and headed north. *That bitch had better not still be there when I arrive.*

CHAPTER 60

Audrey awoke with the sunlight streaming through her cottage skylights. Her bedside clock revealed it was already nine. She turned to the man still peacefully asleep and totally unaware a new day had dawned.

Audrey liked her bed to herself. Only on very rare occasions did she relent and it was usually due to sheer lust. Last night was no exception. Paul was a surprise she hadn't expected. His charm was enticing, his humor contagious and in bed he was deliciously dominating. He was a man who could sexually incite a woman's desire leaving her utterly vulnerable and completely spent. The man's breath was regular and quiet. Quiet being the operative word and the necessary element to any continuing relationship.

Today she was going to inform Poppy and her Uncle Barney, she was closing up the resort in order to do necessary repairs. Unfortunately it meant the man in her bed would also be vacating. She grabbed her dressing gown and turned on the kettle for a pot of tea. The view across the bay revealed a handful of small anchored fishing boats and a large charter yacht heading out to sea. The water was mirror smooth reflecting white puffy clouds and blue sky. A perfect day.

"You sneaked out of bed." She turned to find Paul, fully dressed and looking simply gorgeous. He wrapped his arms around her as she poured hot water into the teapot.

"Careful! You'll make me spill," she laughed as she reached for two cups and popped two slices of multigrain toast in the toaster.

"Did you sleep well?" he muzzled her ear.

"I slept beautifully. Thanks to you." Audrey couldn't believe she was flirting with this man. He made her feel silly and special. "I meant to tell you yesterday I am closing down the business here for a week or so. I have some urgent maintenance that needs to be taken care of. Poppy mentioned you were planning on taking a boat trip anyway."

"Poppy will be disappointed."

"There are some wonderful places to stay in Mangonui and I would be happy to call and make her a reservation if she wants," she offered.

Paul was obviously surprised by the news "And we have just got to know each other."

"I know. You will just have to pursue me from afar." She laughed.

"I had better get over there and relay the sad news. I guess we will be back to check out in an hour or so. Is that OK?"

"Absolutely, take your time."

Audrey knew Poppy would be seriously annoyed when she got the news. What could she do? Nothing. It was turning out to be a wonderful day. She relished the thought of being guest free for a whole week. Soon the summer season would be upon her and this would be her last break. She poured a second cup of tea and headed out to the picnic table in the sun.

As soon as the man relayed the news to Poppy she exploded!

"She said what?" Poppy couldn't believe it. "What audacity! First she destroys all our bloody spy equipment, and now she is throwing us out onto the street! Well fuck her!"

CHAPTER 61

M ei couldn't wait to see Audrey. She was dying to tell her the news about the lawyer. She had hardly slept she was so excited. He called earlier to confirm Steve had no living relatives and had died 'intestate', which, he explained, meant died without a will. He was filing the necessary 'letters of administration' for the estate and said the court would more than likely appoint her as administrator of the estate. Mae was ecstatic. Her lawyer didn't see any problems and would come by tomorrow to have her sign the necessary documents.

Mae heard the trappers on their quad bikes. She liked that the property was a major contributor to saving the kiwi birds. When she heard the doorbell ring she presumed it was the trapper. Opening the door Mei came face to face with her future nightmare. A man, short, stumpy, big bellied, tattooed and leather clad.

"Hello little lady," he said condescendingly. "I am Steve's son, David Williams. Pleased to meet you. I am surprised you are still here. I thought you would've returned to China by now." He was carrying a large duffle bag and, pushing past Mei, he dropped it on her delicate shoes in the foyer and strode brazenly in his heavy black boots into the house.

"I didn't know Steve had a son," was all Mei could think to say. "He said he never married and had no children."

"My father was a shithead! He left my mother, pregnant and desolate forty-three years ago. I guess it 's payback time." David fell back on the leather sofa and put his boots on the armrest. "Thanks Dad. Loving my new digs."

"Why do you think Steve is your Father?"

"My Mother kept a photo of him. Never talked about him. She died a year ago. I found her letters to him. He never responded. I read what he did to you in the papers. I saw old photos of him and recognized him immediately. What about you, pretty lady? How did you meet my father? He lit a cigarette and blew the smoke in her direction.

"We met through a dating agency. I came over here to study and marry your father."

"And now? When are you returning home?"

Mei looked at the man with disgust. He reeked of beer and cigarettes. She walked into the kitchen and returned with a small saucer for his ashtray. "I am not returning. I am staying here."

"That's not going happen. As his only living relative, this is my house, my property and I see I have just inherited a boat, quad and brand-new car. So, pretty lady, I suggest you pack your bags and find another sugar daddy to take you in."

Mei departed to the master bedroom and sat on the edge of the bed looking at her reflection in the dresser mirror. What am I to do? Where can I go? She called her lawyer. "Mr. Morris. It's Mei here. I am in trouble. Steve's son just arrived and said he is moving in here. I don't know what to do."

"He has a son? There is no record of a living son."

"He said Steve walked away from his mother when she was

pregnant. He is sure Steve is his father. He has a photo and letters to prove it."

"He will need to do a DNA test to prove it. But even so, Mei, a de facto partner has priority over children. If you are truly pregnant, then we have a good case for you to own the estate."

"What am I to do? I can't stay here with him here."

"Tell him you are going nowhere, and your lawyer says you have the right to live in the house as his de facto partner."

"I am scared. Mr. Morris. He looks like a gang member."

"Then tell him to leave. Mei. Do you have someone you can call to help you?

"Yes, I will call Audrey next door and ask her."

"Good Mei. I will be there tomorrow. Call me again if you need anything."

"I will. Thanks Mr. Morris."

"Call me Guy,'" he said, and hung up.

Chapter 62

Audrey watched their cars leaving down the long driveway and sighed with relief. She could tell Poppy was infuriated. She paid her bill and left without saying a word. Barney and Paul were more understanding when she explained it was an electrical problem and there would be no power in the cabins for the next week. She lied, of course, and didn't care if they believed her or not. They were gone and she could enjoy a whole week of pure peace and solitude. Paul said he would call her when they returned from their fishing trip.

It was noon before she had finished cleaning the cabins, doing the laundry and refilled the spas. She made lunch, sat at the picnic table on the front lawn and watched the boats and kayaks enjoying the spring day. It was quiet. A couple of native wood pigeons sat on the karaka tree beside her. Tuis sang their melodic tunes and fantails hopped and fluttered beside her on the lawn looking for bugs and nibbles.

"Hello Audrey,"

Audrey jumped. The voice startled the birds causing them to fly in all directions "Mei, I didn't hear you arrive."

"Sorry, I didn't mean to frighten you. But I am in serious trouble, Audrey and I don't know what to do."

"Mei. What's happened?" Audrey looked at the frail girl with swollen eyes and a face still marked by violence.

"Steve has a son. He is awful. He is over at the house. Says he is living there now. Told me to leave."

"Steve has a son? I thought he never married. Had no children. Are you sure he is his son?"

"He said he has letters from Steve to his mother. And a photo. I called my lawyer and he said for me to stay in the house. That I have more rights as Steve's de facto partner than any child."

"You found a lawyer? That is good, Mei. Good work. He will make sure your rights are protected."

"What is this son like?"

"He is horrible. Has tattoos, rides a motorbike, smells dirty. He even looks and acts like his father. Guy said they will make him take a DNA test. But, Audrey, he looks like Steve. I know he is his son. What will I do? I am too scared to stay there with him."

"What did your lawyer say?"

"He said to stay there and ask him to leave. But I am afraid of him."

"Do you want me to come over and talk to him?"

"Would you? That would really help."

"OK. Have you eaten today, Mei?"

"No I am too upset to eat."

"Before we go, you must have something to eat. You need to keep your strength up. You are still healing and it is going to be a tough path ahead. Come on in the kitchen and I will make you a chicken sandwich."

Mei agreed reluctantly. They ate and talked for over an hour. Mei obviously didn't want to return next door.

"I am not sure about the law. But I think you should stay there. If you leave the house, you may jeopardize your de facto relationship status."

The two women headed off down the long, grassed track bordered by bush and separating the two properties.

"I didn't know there was a track between our properties" Mae commented.

"It is used by the trappers." Audrey replied as the house came into view.

CHAPTER 63

Poppy checked the time; it was already getting dark. She had spent the whole day writing in her room at the Mangonui Inn. It was a nice room overlooking Mangonui bay. There were no cooking facilities like in the cabin but restaurants were within walking distance. She was still furious Audrey had kicked her out. How the hell was she supposed to research her book stuck over here in the village?

When her phone rang she was soaking in the bath. It was a pleasant surprise to hear from him.

"Poppy, what are you up to? It is Jimmy Bromley here. Wondering if you would like to catch a bite to eat. I have some news that might interest you."

"What time, where? I have moved into the village. Audrey threw me out."

"She did?" He laughed. "What did you do?"

"Nothing. She has closed the cabins for week for some sort of repairs. Personally, I think she just wanted me gone."

"You are getting paranoid, Poppy. Where are you staying?"

"I'm at the Mangonui Inn. Why don't I meet you at the restaurant bar next door?"

"Done. How does eight sound?"

"See you then." Poppy sunk back in the bubbles and felt a whole lot better. *He said Jimmy Bromley not Detective Inspector Bromley.* It was a sign he was getting personal with her. Did she mind? Not at all. The closer she got to him the better.

Dressed to seduce, Poppy scrutinized her outfit in the mirror meticulously. She had chosen a dress that hugged her body to perfection. Poppy liked to wear high heels - the higher the better. Her perfume was subtle and alluring. Tonight she would seduce Jimmy Bromley. She wondered what news he could possibly have to tell her.

He was sitting at the bar when she entered and seemed to sense she was there. Turning, he greeted her. "Poppy, you look beautiful!"

She wondered how he could explain their association. He, a married man and living in such a tight rural community.

"Thank you." she responded and took the seat beside him.

"I have made dinner reservations at a little restaurant in Kerikeri we have time for just one quick drink." He looked at a clock on the wall of the bar. "Our reservations are for nine o'clock."

Poppy ordered a gin martini with olives. The cocktail glass was chilled to perfection. As she sipped, she looked at the man beside her. He seemed relaxed and remarkably unaffected by the stares the local patrons were giving them. She wondered if he had a reputation for taking young women out to dinner. Was he a player openly cheating on his wife?

"So do you invite strange women to dinner on a regular basis?"

He laughed. "I wouldn't call you strange. More like unique."

"You know what I mean." She leaned closer and whispered in his ear, "I don't want to get you into any trouble."

He blushed. She thought it charming. "Shall we go?" he asked.

The restaurant was enchanting with intimate outside seating surrounded by native and tropical gardens. Fairy lights created a festive ambiance and romantic music floated in the evening breeze. Poppy felt appreciated. It had been quite some time since she was made to feel so special. What a shame this man was married. They chose the duck special and the detective ordered a bottle of Cloudy Bay Sauvignon Blanc. She wondered how he could support his expensive tastes and a family on a policeman's wage.

Poppy was impatient and could resist no longer. "So tell me, Jimmy. What is the news you have to tell me?"

He became serious and leaned toward her. "I received a call today from a friend of mine, Guy Morris. He is acting on behalf of Mei Wong. You remember she was the fiancé of Steve Sutton? Poppy nodded. "Mei is applying to become administrator of Sutton's estate as his de facto partner."

"But she was only with him a few days?"

"Yes. But she is apparently pregnant which gives her legal ownership of his estate."

"Wow. Her husband's death was very advantageous, wasn't it?" Poppy's mind was spinning. "I bet Audrey was involved."

"Now, Poppy. Don't jump to conclusions. I know you were interested in the case and I thought you would see the strange justice in it. The man beats her half to death in a drunkard rage and drowns leaving his mail-order bride to inherit his rather large estate. It makes for good reading don't you think?"

"Why did her lawyer call you?"

"Because I was working on the case, and he wanted to

confirm the incident was an accident and if I had any information that may help to solidify Mei's position."

"And do you?"

"Just that we took a rape kit test when she arrived at the hospital and it proved positive. The DNA matched Sutton's DNA. Mei would need to take another test in a couple of weeks to confirm the pregnancy, but Guy said it looks pretty positive at this stage."

Poppy remained silent. She just knew Audrey was involved somehow. She would pay Mei a friendly visit tomorrow. She reached over and took the detective's hand and smiled. "That is wonderful news for Mei. I hope she gets it all. What wonderful payback for all she has gone through. I guess the man had no living relatives?

"Apparently not. Never married. Parents dead and no siblings."

Poppy was itching to get back in her room so she could research the legalities of de facto relationships in probate.

He walked to the door of the Inn and waited for her to invite him in. She didn't. "I had a wonderful evening, Jimmy. Thank you so much."

"We must do it again soon." Disappointment showed on his face.

Poppy was already inside and heading for her room when the detective returned to his car. She had more important things on her mind. Damn Audrey. What am I missing?

CHAPTER 64

A udrey and Mei removed their shoes and entered the house cautiously. "David." Mei called getting no reply.

"His bike is here. He can't have gone far." Audrey said going from room to room.

"I will check to see if he has taken the car or quad bike out," Mei said, as she headed for the shed.

"He's taken the car. I can't believe it. Just taken the car as if it is his. What should I do?"

"I don't think there is anything you can do until your lawyer gets it sorted out. You call me when he gets back and I will come over."

"I am frightened of him, Audrey. He scares me. If I ask him to leave he may beat me or throw me out."

"If he makes trouble you need to call the police straight away. Promise?"

"Can you just stay a little while?" Mei begged.

Audrey stayed until the sun set and it was getting dark. "You should go to your room and stay there tonight. Lock the door. If he tries anything, you call me immediately. OK?"

Audrey arrived back at Tiromoana and opened a bottle of wine. She was glad her life was less complicated. Poor Mei. At least Audrey had done her a favor. Damn the bloody son arriving on her doorstep. Tomorrow morning she would go over and check Mei was all right. Hopefully the guy went out on the binge and is lying drunk in a gutter somewhere. Wouldn't that be perfect?

It was after nine when Audrey awoke. Sleeping in was a luxury. No guests! Heaven! She rolled over and slept another hour oblivious to the needs of her new neighbor who was still in her bedroom with the door locked listening in fear to her unwelcome guest stomping through the house in his heavy boots.

The ringing of her phone called her into action as she leaned across to answer it. "Hello. Tiromoana Cabins. Can I help you?" she mumbled sleepily. "Mei!" She bolted upright remembering her promise. "What is it? Are you all right? OK. I'll be right over." She grabbed her jeans and sweatshirt, brushed her hair up into a ponytail and headed for the door. The track was a good distance between the two houses and she made it in record time. There was no sign of Mei. She knocked at the door and heard heavy footsteps approaching. She was prepared.

"Yes?" The short, muscled, tattooed man stood defiantly in the open doorway. "What do you want?"

"I am your neighbor, Audrey Wetherby. I am pleased to meet you," she offered her outstretched hand with a smile.

"David Williams," he replied grudgingly.

"I promised Mei I'd take her lunch today. Is she around?"

The man looked surprised. "She's not here. I guess she left. Nothing to keep her here."

"She called me only a few minutes ago. Said she was ready to go."

"Nope. Haven't seen her. I've just got up myself. Can't help ya." He closed the door in her face.

Audrey didn't move. What a shithead! She dialed Mei's cell phone. There was no reply. Where the hell is she? She rang the doorbell and waited. The man never answered. She decided to walk around the house and see if she could see Mei anywhere. Every room had floor to ceiling windows. There was one room with the curtains pulled closed. She knocked on the ranch sliders. She heard moaning inside. She tried to open the door - it wouldn't budge. She called softly "Mei, is that you? Open the door." She heard movement and the door latch snapped open. She slid open the door and was shocked. Mei lay in a heap by the door. Beaten and bruised. Audrey held her in her arms. "Mei did he do this to you?" Mei nodded. "I'll call the police." Audrey reached for her phone.

"No. Please don't," Mei begged. "I don't want to go to the hospital again. Will you take me to your place?"

"But you can't walk down the track like this and I don't want to leave you here while I get my car."

"I will be all right. Just hurry."

Audrey quietly closed the screen door and made her way back through the track to get her car. She had no idea what the man would do when she returned to pick up Mei. Men like him were easy to make disappear. They were stupid and vulnerable. A bottle of whisky with a splash of GHB always made them more docile and easier to handle. She had no qualms sedating him. Better to be safe than sorry.

CHAPTER 65

Poppy saw it was almost noon and headed up highway 10 towards the small seaside settlement of Hihi. She had stopped at the market to pick up flowers and fresh strawberries – a housewarming present. The morning blue skies had turned to grey. Storm clouds were brewing on the horizon. Large spits of rain hit her windshield forcing her to turn on the wipers. As she reached the Hihi beach, the ocean was swollen with white caps and waves were crashing over the rocks onto the road. The wind was strong and angry. The storm had come on so quickly it had taken her by surprise. She wished she had decided to make this visit another day. She wasn't dressed for walking around in this weather and Mei lived in such an isolated spot on the peninsula she had no idea if she could park close to the house.

Finding Mei's driveway, she headed up the long windy gravel road towards the large modern home on the cliff in the distance. The trees were swaying in the wind. She saw the trackers hut. It looked closed for the day. She guessed the weather was not conducive to kiwi care. Parked in front of the house she noticed a Range Rover, quad bike, boat and kayaks all lined up in the large shed close by. She felt a pang of envy knowing Mei was inheriting all of this after only a few days of knowing Steve Sutton. Why couldn't she find financial security so easily?

Parking her car she made her way to the front door and rang the bell. There was no answer. She knocked a few times. Still no answer. Damn. No-one was home. She walked around the house looking in the windows. She was on a mission. A while later she thought she heard a motorbike in the distance and realized it was coming from over at Tiromoana. It was time to go. She could feel the cold wind bite into her bare arms and legs. She returned to her car, turned on the heater and looked out at the ocean watching in fascination as huge menacing rain clouds formed overhead. Then it came - the rain. Streams of water began gouging new pathways through the gravel drive. Deep puddles formed in crevices and ditches. Poppy realized she needed to get down onto the main road before the flooding became serious. She turned her car towards the main driveway and headed out onto Peninsula Road. A motorbike came speeding out of Audrey's driveway almost hitting her and forcing her to slide into the shallow ditch. Shit! She braked. The rain had reduced visibility to almost zero. Slowly she made her way down Peninsula Road and out onto the main highway.

She was back in her room looking out the window when she saw them - Mei and Audrey. She would recognize Audrey's car anywhere. A light blue Rav4. They were driving slowly down the Mangonui waterfront. Where are they going in this weather? Who was that on the motorbike leaving Audrey's at high speed?

CHAPTER 66

Detective Inspector Bromley was puzzled. He had told Poppy last night about Guy representing Mei. What he hadn't told her is Guy's concern about the sudden appearance of Sutton's alleged son. Bromley had agreed to do a background check on him. David Williams was indeed a bad seed. Known for his violent behavior, he had a string of convictions including attempted rape on a minor, physical abuse of a prostitute, theft, meth distribution and numerous drunk driving violations. Williams was a long-time member of the Head Hunters chapter based in Glen Innes in Auckland.

The Head Hunters motorcycle gang was also prevalent in Northland. Bromley didn't want any more trouble. This David Williams was not welcome in his territory. Guy had asked him to look in on Mei. Apparently, Williams had turned up at Sutton's house and just moved in. Mei could be in danger.

All morning Bromley had been calling Sutton's phone getting no answer. He wondered if the phone had already been disconnected. His weekly meeting at the Whangarei branch was in a couple of hours and he wouldn't be returning to Mangonui until late afternoon. If he hadn't talked to Mei by then he would make a quick stop on his way back.

Dinner last night with Poppy was going really well until he mentioned Mei's pregnancy and the opportunity of inheriting Sutton's estate. It was like a switch flicked. She became despondent, obsessed, almost wanting to accuse Audrey for Sutton's death again. What was wrong with the girl? He had hoped to spend more time with her.

The weather had not improved during the afternoon. The trip back from Whangarei was slow, due to the heavy deluge of rain. He stopped twice to help motorists having difficulties crossing the flooded rural roads. He decided to head up to Hihi before returning to his office.

The sun had already set by the time he reached Mei's. He was surprised to see it in total darkness. No lights inside or out. He walked around the house peering in windows. Two rooms had closed curtains. He knocked on the locked ranch sliders. Nothing. He had noticed a Harley parked in the shed next to the Range Rover. If Williams was not at the house and had not taken his bike or Sutton's Ute where was he? The weather was atrocious there was no way Williams would be wandering around the property unless he was checking for flood damage. Where was Mei? He knocked again. Nothing. Bromley returned to his car and headed over to Audrey's next door. Maybe Mei had taken shelter over there.

As he drove up the driveway towards Audrey's cottage, he noticed there were no lights on there either. Tiromoana was in darkness. He pulled into the car park as his radio crackled into action.

"Where are you Inspector? We have an area wide power outage and getting calls of slips and road accidents. Are you close-by? We are heading to an accident on the bridge by Folgers Road."

He immediately turned around and headed to the scene. "I'm five minutes away." No time to check on Mei. Bromley knew it would be a long night. He hadn't noticed the faint flicker of candlelight in Audrey's cottage as he sped off into the storm.

CHAPTER 67

When Audrey went to collect Mei, she was alone.
"He took the quad bike and headed down towards the beach," she told her. "I heard him leave just a few minutes ago. Hurry before he comes back."

Audrey quickly bundled Mei into her car. Mei had already packed a small bag. She looked so vulnerable. Hurt and afraid.

"You know I should take you to a doctor and have him look at your face. It looks bad." Audrey was concerned.

"I am fine. It looks worse than it is. I just need to sleep. I am so tired. I have been awake most of the night."

"Why did he attack you?" Audrey asked as she drove her to Tiromoana.

"I told him my lawyer said I had preferred rights to the property as his de facto partner and he should leave. I was so scared, Audrey. He went crazy and just started attacking me. Called me a whore. Told me to go home. I thought he was going to kill me."

"We should call the police."

"Please Audrey, I just want to rest."

Audrey settled Mei into her cottage. They were both dripping wet from running through the rain. "A hot bath and a change of clothes will make you feel a lot better. Then we can decide what to do."

They heard his bike through the storm. Loud and menacing.

"What the fuck!" he shouted. "Don't think you are getting penny of my father's property. You bitches! Fuck you!" The man kicked at the locked screen doors with his heavy boots. She pulled the curtains closed in his face which only made him kick all the harder. "I know you are in there. I don't wanna see your fucking Chink face ever again! Go back to Chinatown bitch!" he bellowed.

Audrey heard him start his motorbike and listened to the roar as he sped down her driveway and back up the driveway next door. She knew he was coming back. His sort did. They didn't stop until they had eliminated anyone or anything in their way.

"We must get out of here." Audrey grabbed her car keys. "He will be back."

"Mei was petrified. "He'll kill me."

Not if I get to him first. "Grab your bag Mei. We are leaving."

Audrey had one thing in mind. She wanted Mei to be put into a safe place. There was no doubt David Williams was on a mission and she needed some serious alone time to deal with him.

Her first stop was the police station. Detective Inspector Bromley was not there when they arrived. A volunteer was working the front desk. "He had a meeting in Whangarei," he explained "He is expected back shortly." Audrey decided to check Mei into a little bed and breakfast close by. She would be safe there. She told Mei she would be back tomorrow to check on her and headed out into the storm.

Audrey loved bad weather as much as she loved to take revenge on a shithead like David Williams. It was a perfect storm.

She hoped by now he had finished off the bottle of whisky she had left earlier in the empty booze cabinet. She could tell he was a boozer. To be safe she had spiked the bottles of beer in the fridge also. With any luck Mr. David Williams was passed out on the floor.

She parked her car at Tiromoana, grabbed her gumboots and rain gear and walked the long grassy track. Having taken Mei's keys to the house, she let herself in quietly, locking the door behind her. David's bike had been parked in the shed. She had checked. The rain pelted loudly on the iron roof drowning out any sound she, or anyone, would make. She noticed the empty whisky bottle on the kitchen bench surrounded by dirty dishes. Open empty cans of baked beans indicated the man had enjoyed his last meal.

She smelled him before she saw him - spread across the bed, fully dressed – still in his boots. Audrey stayed in the doorway of the guest bedroom watching and listening. The storm was sending airborne branches and twigs crashing against the windows. The rain pelted with fury. Approaching the comatose tattooed beast of a man with disgust she felt his weak pulse. His beer-soaked open mouth exposed missing teeth and dripping drawl. The man's backpack was in the corner of the room. She knew what she was looking for. It didn't take a genius to know he would have his own stash of drugs. She injected a lethal concoction into his vein and waited for a response. Nothing. He was too far gone. She struggled to roll him over smothering his face in the folds of the pillow then sat on the bed beside him listening to the sounds of the wind and rain and waited. Finally his pulse was still. Mr. David Williams would not be residing at his father's house after all.

She closed the bedroom curtains and ensured the ranch sliders were locked. It might be days before the body was found.

As she turned the key to the lock the front door, she heard a car heading up the driveway. She darted out of sight heading for the track entrance. She watched through the dense bush as a police car pulled into the parking area by the front door. It was Detective Inspector Bromley. He knocked on the door and called out to Mei. Audrey returned down the track through the rain. Strong winds spewed branches like twigs across her path. A large fallen tree forced her to detour off the main track back to her cottage.

Inside, she stripped naked and grabbed her robe. She was cold and wet. The lights were out. Another power cut. She found the lamp and lit candles and sat in the flickering glow and waited. She knew the detective would call on her. Getting no response next door, he would presume Mei was with her. It would be the perfect alibi. She wished she could have dried her hair, but no power meant no hair dryer. She wasn't disappointed, within minutes she heard his car pulling into her parking lot. The rain was constant – beating harder on the tin roof. She shivered. She heard his car drive away. Damn! Why? She may as well light the fire and get warm.

Chapter 68

Barney and Paul saw the weather approaching from the north and headed back to the safety of the Mangonui harbor. They made it back before dark and called Poppy, who arranged rooms for them at her Inn.

Paul was eager to meet up with Audrey. She had been on his mind while he was at sea. He was disappointed he wouldn't be staying at Tiromoana tonight.

Poppy was bursting with everything she had learned about Mei's claim on Sutton's estate. "Can you believe it? She lucked out big time. She'll be a wealthy woman. I just know Audrey had something to do with it."

"There is no way Audrey would have known Mei was pregnant. From what you say, it is also very early and the pregnancy test may not be one hundred percent."

"They seem to be thick as thieves since Steve Sutton's death. I saw them only a few hours ago in the village together." Poppy looked really smug. "Anyway, I will have proof this time."

"What have you done, Poppy?" Barney looked surprised.

"I just put a spy camera at Sutton's house yesterday when I went to visit Mei. She wasn't there.

"This is becoming an obsession, Poppy. You need to stop it. Your brother's death was awful. A tragedy. But it is time for you to get on with your life. Leave it alone. Tomorrow I want you to go over there and remove the camera. The poor girl, Mei, has gone through enough without you making matters worse."

"I only put one at the front door to see who was coming and going." Poppy was disappointed her uncle didn't share her same passion for proving Audrey's murdering persona. She needed concrete evidence for her book. "If you insist. I will go over tomorrow. If anyone is there, I won't be able to just say; 'Oh, excuse me. I would like to pick up the spy camera I left here yesterday.'

"I will call Audrey and see what I can find out," said Paul. "I will invite them both out to lunch if that will help."

"There you are. No excuse now," said Barney.

CHAPTER 69

The Northland chapter of the Head Hunters Motorcycle Gang heard Williams was in their territory. The news was out he was going to be inheriting a large estate in Hihi and that was reason for a serious fucking celebration in their books. When numerous calls and messages were left unanswered they decided to pay him a visit. It was party time!

The continuous sound of motorbikes making their way up the gravel road past Tiromoana startled Audrey who was clearing away the debris left from last night's storm. Motorbike gangs always made her nervous. As a small child growing up in Christchurch, her parents always warned her about them. "Keep away from bikers they are very, very dangerous." She didn't know why they were dangerous; she just knew she shouldn't piss them off. She wondered if killing one of their notorious members would warrant pissing them off. *I guess it would.*

Last night Audrey had celebrated with a bottle of wine and another perfectly positioned star on her ceiling. As she lay on the soft, carpeted floor, staring at the brightly lit ceiling, she felt at peace. Mei was safe and another shithead got what he deserved.

She felt vindicated, even righteous. Sometimes fate just needs an extra push.

The noise of revving Harleys next door disturbed the usual silence of her rural paradise. She knew there would be no answer. They would eventually leave. She was wrong. They had obviously decided to stay and party. She could hear them cheering. Bikers, men in black and red with skull devil logos and patches. Some known rapists, killers and druggies. Others just Harley freaks wanting to belong. Audrey thought it rather ironic the Head Hunters were celebrating their mate's good fortune at inheriting the property, while he was lying face down in his own drawl, dead as a headless chicken.

By noon she had enough of the drunkard brawl next door and headed off into Mangonui to visit with Mei. She felt great. Sunshine and blue skies had warmed the ground and dried the puddles, leaving everything looking green and fresh.

As she made her way down Peninsula Road, past the Motor Camp, she spotted Poppy heading up towards Tiromoana. She waved her down. "Poppy, where are you off to?"

"Thought I would stop by and visit with Mei and see how she is doing?"

"She is not staying there at the moment. She is in Mangonui. I am just on my way to see her. Follow me," Audrey offered.

Poppy had no choice. She turned her car around and followed Audrey into the Mangonui village.

Parking her car outside the Bed and Breakfast, Audrey checked her messages. There were three from Paul inviting her and Mei to lunch. Damn! Oh well. She would call him later.

CHAPTER 70

Detective Inspector Bromley received a call from the Motor Camp at Hihi complaining of the noise generating from up the Peninsula. "At least fifty motorbikes passed here on their way up there this morning," the owner said. "Looked like one of the Northland gangs."

"It is not the police's responsibility to handle noise ordinance. You have to call the Council. But I was planning on heading up that way anyway today so I will check it out and get back to you." Bromley had been the local cop for a number of years now and keeping your neighborhood happy was as important as keeping them safe. It paid off in the long run.

Early afternoon he headed up Peninsula Road. As soon as he reached the entranceway to Tiromoana he could hear the commotion. It was coming from old Sutton's place next door. He guessed Williams had invited his Harley friends to a celebration. He turned into the driveway and headed towards the house. He was greeted by a large mob of beer-drinking, partying guys, obviously too drunk to go anywhere. He could see Sutton's boat down on the beach with half a dozen guys getting ready to go take it out. They looked surprised to see him. Bromley knew many of the guys. They were mostly a harmless lot.

"Is Williams around?" he asked a particularly heavyset biker.

"Nope. He's not home. We have been waiting for him all day."

"You haven't seen him all day?"

"Nope. He's not answering his phone either."

"When was the last time anyone talked to him?" asked Bromley sensing something wasn't right.

"No-one has talked to him for a couple of days. A mate talked to him when he arrived here. Invited us for a bash."

"Has anyone looked inside?" Bromley asked.

"Can't get in. It's all locked up," the guy said.

"That hasn't stopped you in the past." Bromley said wryly. "I think we should check inside."

Within minutes a swarm of bikers followed the detective through the house. Dirty dishes on the bench, empty whisky bottles, empty beer bottles and the smell of death permeated throughout the house. The central heating had been turned on high and it was just a matter of following the stench to discover the bloated body of David Williams lying facedown on the master bed.

Bromley called for back up and asked the bikers to vacate the property immediately. They obliged with sincere respect for their fellow gang member. He heard them start their bikes and with a roar they were off leaving him alone at the scene and wondering how the hell Williams ended up dead and alone in his father's house. A father he had never met.

He wondered if Mei had anything to do with his death. Where was she? Her clothes were still on the bed in the master bedroom. He wondered if Williams was already dead when he knocked on the door the evening before. That explained why his bike was in the shed and he had not answered the door.

When forensics arrived he left them to it and headed back to the station. They felt he had only been dead for about twenty-four hours and it was the heat in the house that caused the body to decompose so quickly.

As Bromley drove along the Mangonui waterfront towards the station, he was shocked to see Poppy, Audrey and Mei eating lunch at the corner restaurant. He parked his car and went to join them.

CHAPTER 71

Paul Riley was disappointed Audrey hadn't returned his calls. He didn't know if his fascination with her was the possibility she was a serial killer, like Poppy believed, or that she was just so elusive and alluring. Either way, he was determined to track her down.

He should have checked in with Poppy but had been focused on finding Audrey. He had tried Tiromoana but there was no sign of her there. A commotion was going on next door and he decided to head back into Mangonui. As he headed down the main street he saw Audrey, Poppy, Detective Inspector Bromley and a young woman seated at a roadside table. He parked and went to join them.

Audrey stood to greet him as he walked towards their table. "Paul what a surprise. I just picked up your messages."

Paul looked at Poppy. "I didn't expect to see you here."

Audrey looked over at the young woman "Paul this is Mei. She is living next door to me."

Of course Paul knew who she was. "Hello Mei, nice to meet you."

Audrey said, "You haven't met Detective Inspector Bromley have you Paul."

The men shook hands.

"Paul is a friend of Poppy's and was staying at Tiromoana," she explained.

"I was just leaving," the detective as he stood to give Paul his seat at the table. He looked at Mei. "When you finish lunch can you stop by the station, I have some more questions."

"Can Audrey come with me?" she asked.

"Yes. If you prefer."

"So what did the detective want?" asked Paul.

"He found David Williams dead in Mei's house." Poppy said excitedly. "Can you believe it? Dead! Said he died yesterday afternoon. I was at the house at noon and his bike wasn't there. He must have died shortly after I was there." Poppy gave Paul a knowing look. She knew she had to get back to the house and remove the spy camera. This was it! She would have proof! She didn't even question that Audrey murdered the man. This time they would have to believe her.

Paul knew exactly what Poppy was thinking. He didn't approve of the way she was stalking Audrey. He just hoped Poppy would be proved wrong and Audrey had nothing to do with it.

Audrey and Mei finished their coffee, excused themselves and took the short walk to the police station on the corner.

Poppy was itching to read the memory card from the camera but the detective said the whole property would be cordoned off and under police surveillance for at least a couple more days. She would just have to wait. There was no way she was going to tell the detective the camera was there. She wanted to look at the photos first. If her photos got into police hands she was sure she wouldn't be able to sell them to the media and promote her new book. Finally, she would expose Audrey for whom she really was – a serial killer and, at the same time, make a fortune doing it.

CHAPTER 72

Audrey couldn't shake the feeling Poppy knew something she didn't. The news David Williams' body had been found was not surprising knowing a gang of bikers had invaded the property. As the man was a druggy and a boozer it wouldn't be out of character to find him full of drugs and whisky and smothered in his own drool. She had seen a sign of sudden relief on Mei's face when she heard the news. Her troubles would be over – she would most likely inherit it all. Good for her.

She was curious to know what questions Detective Inspector Bromley had for Mei. After all, they had explained Mei left the house earlier in the day of question, while Steve was out on the quad bike. Audrey was her witness. Mei's fresh wounds proved Steve had beaten her. She wondered if the Detective thought it might have given Mei a motive for killing the man. But Mei was petite and obviously intimidated by the biker surely there would be no doubt she was a victim in the situation. There was also a record of their visit to the police station the same day. She presumed once the time of death was established, it would eliminate Mei from any suspicion.

The detective was pleased Mei was staying in downtown Mangonui as the police would be treating the house as a crime scene until the death could be established as an accident. It looked like an overdose combined with suffocation – but a toxicology report would give a clearer indication as to what Williams had taken prior to his death.

Mei signed her written statement and Audrey walked back to the Bed and Breakfast with her. Mei's injuries were still troubling her and she just wanted to spend the rest of the day resting.

Audrey returned to Tiromoana, dying to see what was going on next door. She changed into black sweats and black hooded t-shirt and headed down the track to satisfy her curiosity. She wasn't disappointed. The place was buzzing with police. She stood back in the bushes and watched from a distance. An ambulance was parked by the front door indicating the body had not been removed yet. It had been almost two hours since Detective Inspector Bromley said he had found the body. She guessed leaving the central heating on high would have caused increased decomposition. She wondered what the delay was. Then she saw the body, already bagged and on a stretcher being carried to the ambulance. Two police cars followed the ambulance down the driveway, leaving one police car still at the scene. She waited a while and realized the police were going to be staying there. There was nothing more she needed to see and she returned back to the cottage.

He was standing at the cottage door looking gorgeous. "Paul, you never cease to surprise me. You are just in time for wine and sunset.

Sitting at the picnic table overlooking the bay they talked and laughed and told funny stories. Audrey liked this man. He smelled so good. He was funny and exciting and so damn sexy.

"Are you staying for dinner?" she asked.

"Am I invited?"

"If you like shrimp stir-fry, you are."

"And I even have some wonderful Sauvignon Blanc in a chiller in my Ute – I'll just go get it." Paul walked out to his car and checked his cell phone. It was Poppy. *"Can you get the camera?"* He texted back *"Not yet."* Damn Poppy. He had promised her he would try and remove the camera. He would wait until dark.

It was almost midnight when Audrey and Paul fell asleep in each other's arms.

CHAPTER 73

Fuck Audrey! Poppy had stayed awake most of the night waiting for Paul's text telling her he had the cameras. Not a bloody thing! She had knocked at his room and there was no reply. She figured he had spent the night with her. *Fuck!* She made a coffee in her room and calmed herself. After all, Paul was her bait and Audrey had taken it. It was just a matter of time and they would have the photos and the proof.

Poppy decided to risk it. She left a note for her uncle and Paul, and drove to Hihi. She would park her car down at the Hihi township and walk along the waterfront. She knew Honeymoon Beach at Tiromoana bordered the two properties. She could climb up the ridge between the two properties and check to see if the police had gone.

It was a steep climb. She found an old overgrown track blocked now with gorse and brush making the path difficult. A slip had eaten a large gouge in the hillside forcing her to climb on hands and knees across the crevice to reach the edge of the Tiromoana property. Sutton's house was on the adjoining ridge in the distance. She found a grass track leading between the two properties. Within a few minutes she was standing on the edge of the bush only fifty feet from the house. There was no-one in sight. She listened. Silence. They must have cordoned off the entranceway at the road. She made a run for the front door her heart pounding half expecting to hear someone shout at her. No-one did. She reached up to where she had hidden the camera and couldn't feel it. She stood on tiptoes. *Fuck! It's gone!* She looked everywhere. Had it fallen? Had the police found it? Had Paul already taken it? *Damn! What now?* She heard a car coming up the long driveway and dashed for the track. It was the police. She had no choice. She had to leave.

Chapter 74

Paul sat at the small table in his room looking at Poppy's camera. The motion camera took three photos in sequence. As he downloaded the photos into his computer he saw they were all dated in chronological order. The first photos showed a short stocky man entering the house at 12.42pm. He guessed it was Williams. Then he saw her, *Fuck! It's Audrey*, entering the house with a key at 5.23pm The next three photos saw her leaving at 5.58pm. *What was she doing in the house for thirty-five minutes* At 6.02pm Detective Inspector Bromley was standing at the front door. He returned at 6.08pm and rang the bell for the second time. No-one answered the door. He checked the date and all the photos took place on the day of William's death. *Fuck! She was there!* The next set of photos was dated the following day at 10.02am. A group of biker-type guys were standing at the door. No-one answered. He watched as the detective and a group of guys entered through the front door. It was 12.30pm the following day. As he opened each set of photos he saw the police coming and going, the body being carried out and more police. Everything was documented. *Shit! Was Poppy right? Did Audrey kill Williams?*

The only reason he got Poppy's camera was to see for himself what it revealed. He was curious, intrigued. Now he wished he hadn't done it. Should he take the photos to the police? Should he confront Audrey and ask her why she had gone over there? Why did she have a key? Maybe the previous owner had hired her to take care of the property? Mei may have asked her to pick up some of her clothes? There could be a thousand reasons why she would go over to her neighbor's house. This was a remote rural area and neighbors often took care of each other's properties when they were absent. Williams could have left from another door? Or was he already dead when she arrived at the house? Did she kill him? The thoughts ran around and around in his head.

Last night he was convinced Audrey had nothing to do with any of the crimes Poppy was researching. She was sweet, funny, intelligent and as open as a book. He smiled remembering how good it felt to be inside her. Tasting her. Smelling her. *There's no way she could murder anyone.*

One thing was for sure – he wasn't going to give Poppy the camera. Maybe she would think the police had confiscated it. He looked at the time, it was already six thirty. He was late meeting Barney. A day out on the open sea would be a nice distraction.

CHAPTER 75

A udrey awoke to find him gone and a note on the
table.

My Sweet Audrey,
Thanks for such a wonderful evening.
I promised Barney I'd go out fishing with him at dawn.
We should be back before dark.
Hope you can join me for dinner,
Paul.

She felt wonderful! Paul was not like the men she had known
in her past. He was kind, thoughtful, nonjudgmental. He was,
actually perfect. Her body felt young and vibrant, her skin
glowed, her hair shone with a new luster. Today she would enjoy
the day with no guests to disturb her. The days were getting
warmer. She changed into her swimsuit and headed down to
Honeymoon Beach. The track to the beach was well hidden
from the shore. As she reached the opening to the beach she
glimpsed a woman attempting to climb the ridge on the other

side of the beach. *No. It can't be. It's bloody Poppy. What the hell is she doing?* Audrey watched the woman clumsily grabbing at branches and scrambling through the overgrown trail. Why was she not taking the usual track from the beach up to Tiromoana? Was she trying to get to the house next door? There was only one way to find out. Audrey waited until Poppy was out of sight then she returned up the main track and waited for Poppy at the top of the ridge. Finally, she saw her, heading in the direction of Sutton's house. She followed her at a safe distance.

Audrey was surprised to find no sign of the police at her neighbor's house. Poppy was obviously surprised too, as she watched and waited before dashing to the front door. Audrey watched Poppy wondering why she didn't knock or ring the bell. Then she realized Poppy was searching for something above the door. She watched her reaching high behind a rafter in the entranceway then, after a few minutes, gave up obviously defeated. What the hell was she looking for? Then Audrey's heart sank. She had planted a camera there. But why? What did she expect to find? Did the police find it first? Did they now know she had gone into the house on the day Williams died? *Fuck! Fuck! Fuck!*

Audrey turned and jogged the long grassy track back to Tiromoana. She didn't want to confront Poppy. What could she say? She needed time to think. *Damn Poppy! Why can't she just, fucking, leave me alone!!*

CHAPTER 76

Detective Inspector Bromley looked at the forensics report. Williams had a high level of alcohol in his system. That was no surprise. He also had an unusual mixture of barbiturates, meth and various other drugs in his blood. The same drugs had been found in his belongings at the scene. It would appear he had taken a fatal dose, combined with the alcohol, and literally suffocated in his pillow. The coroner signed his death certificate as accidental death due to drug overdose. Case closed.

Bromley was pleased he didn't have another murder on his hands. Poppy had put doubts in his mind about Audrey. He was glad he could tell her it was simply an accidental death. He was also pleased Mei would not have to go through more trauma. She had already been through enough.

He called Poppy with the good news.

"Poppy, where are you?"

Poppy had almost reached the water's edge after scrambling down the bank. She was out of breath and stopped to answer her phone. "I am just taking a walk along the beach."

"Perfect day for it. I just wanted to tell you the good news. I have just received Williams' forensics report and it would appear his death was due to an accidental drug overdose. The drugs found in his system were the same drugs he had in his bag at the scene." There was a long pause. "Poppy, are you still there?"

Shit! "Yes, I am here. So you are closing the case?"

"There is no case, Poppy. Just an unfortunate accident. The guy was well known as an alcoholic and heavy drug user. He just shot up one too many times."

Poppy stopped to rest on a large rock on the shore. "I see."

"You sound disappointed. I thought you would be pleased. I know you were worried about Mei. We thought for a moment she had a strong motive for seeing him dead. I am just about to call her. Bye Poppy."

"Bye Jimmy." Poppy didn't move. She watched the water lapping gently at her feet. The cold water felt good. What did he mean she was worried about Mei? She never suspected Mei. It was Audrey she suspected.

He never mentioned the camera. Did he have it?

When the detective gave Mei the good news, he could tell she was relieved. Nothing was stopping her from going forward to claim Sutton's estate. He told Mei, if she needed any help from him, he would be pleased to give it.

Bromley picked up Williams' file and marked it "Case Closed" and threw it in his out-box.

CHAPTER 77

Mei shared the good news with Audrey. The two celebrated over a bottle of champagne. Mei's wounds were healing well. The swelling had subsided leaving just red welts on her check bone and chin.

"My ribs still hurt when I laugh," she chuckled. "Only I didn't know until now."

"So, he said the case is closed?" Audrey confirmed.

"Yes. I have called Guy and told him the good news. He couldn't believe it. He is coming to see me again tomorrow. He really is very kind," she said, blushing.

"Oh Mei. You fancy him," Audrey teased her.

"I am sure he is not interested in me."

"And why not? You are a beautiful girl and now you are going to be a rich one too." Audrey poured more champagne into their empty glasses. "Here's to love and good fortune," she toasted.

"To love and good fortune."

"You know Mei, the other day I popped over to the house to pick up some more of your things." She handed Mei a bag full of clothes Audrey had taken from her suitcase in the guest bedroom. "In all the fuss I forgot I had them. I know you didn't have time to grab much when we left that day."

"Oh Audrey, thank you. You are wonderful! But the detective said I could return back to the house today. Do you think you could drop me off after lunch?"

"That's great news! Of course I'll take you."

Audrey hoped her confession of stopping by the house to pick up Mei's clothes would satisfy any questions the police may have if she was ever asked. Now the case was closed, she doubted the subject would ever arise. But her gut told her it wasn't over yet. Someone had photos. She was sure of it. But who?

They opened the front door to a kitchen full of dirty dishes and a faint odor of death. Audrey checked the guest bedroom and discovered the police had removed all the bedding. The room was reasonably tidy. They had removed all his belongings. There was no sign David Williams had ever slept in the room. The women noticed his Harley was also gone. Maybe the bikers took it, or the police. They didn't care. He was gone.

Mei opened all the sliding doors and let the late afternoon sun shine its warm rays on the cold white walls of the empty house. Audrey felt a shiver run down her spine. The house gave her the creeps. She helped Mei clean the kitchen and left her to soak in a hot bath and enjoy her home for the first time without any fear of being disturbed.

As soon as Audrey walked into her cottage she checked her messages. Paul had called. "Audrey, something's come up. Hope I can take a rain check on dinner tonight. Call you tomorrow." *Shit!*

CHAPTER 78

Paul had returned to the Inn earlier than expected. The fish weren't biting and he wanted to get back to show Barney the photos from Sutton's house. He had confided in Barney expressing his dilemma regarding what to do with the photos. The more he thought about Audrey's visit to the house during the time of Williams' death, the more it worried him. Barney agreed. The coincidence of her being in the house at the same time was suspect, to say the least. Poppy had shared with Barney her concerns regarding the sheer number of murders Audrey Wetherby was either witness to or within close proximity to the crimes.

Barney had put a call in to a mate who worked at the Kaikohe prison. He'd just got back to him with some very interesting information regarding a prior corrections officer, Ben Williams who was arrested for the notorious cocaine smuggling heist that happened a few years ago in Hihi.

Barney told Paul "There's talk in the jail that a woman, Audrey, owned the cabin resort where the men were staying. Rumor has it she was responsible for the series of murders that took place. One of the murders was the corrections officer's ex wife. They say Audrey was having an affair with her and when the woman dumped her, she got rid of her. The cops found most of the drugs, but someone got away with a pretty stash. The gangs were infuriated that the Mexican drug cartel, which was responsible for bringing the cocaine into New Zealand, was working with a chain of brothels to distribute the drugs, and not them. They say it was Audrey who killed the owner of the Brothels, Frankie Perkins, and got away with the missing cocaine."

"If it was Audrey who did all these murders, why isn't she in jail?" Paul couldn't believe what he was hearing.

"She is a smart son of a bitch. She framed her dead lover, Joan Williams and got away with everything."

"Fuck! How many murders does Poppy think she is responsible for?"

"A Black Power member, Hemi Heke, is doing time for a murder in the same jail. Rumor in the jail is that Audrey was responsible for the two murders he got convicted for."

"This is big! And Poppy put all of this together?"

"Yes, she has been working on her book ever since her brother was killed. He was hired to investigate Audrey, apparently. He had spoken to Poppy not long before he was killed. He had been staying at the Hihi Motor Camp."

"Shit. Why was he investigating Audrey?"

"His friend, Higgins, a cop, believed Audrey was responsible for her parents death when she was just a teenager. It was never proven. He was also found dead, the cop, that is – hit his head fishing off Audrey's private beach."

"I am glad we all got out of there. Poppy's life could be in danger. Our lives could be in danger. Fuck! If she finds out that you have been digging into her past, you are dead, mate!" Paul thought about his dinner invitation tonight. What the hell was he going to do? Cancel? Say he needed an early night? "I am supposed to be having dinner with her later." He told Barney.

"I'll call Poppy. Fill her in. She's going to be furious you took her camera and didn't tell her."

"I didn't believe her. About Audrey, I mean. I thought Audrey was completely innocent."

"You're not alone there. I thought it was all in Poppy's head. Now I know differently."

CHAPTER 79

Hemi Heke heard the news about David Williams' death. The Head Hunters and Black Power gangs were both in the meth trade and shared their prevalence in Northland. As soon as Hemi heard David Williams had died in Hihi, he knew that bitch, Audrey Wetherby, had something to do with it.

Their two gangs were dealing with a dispute over a recent meth raid. Blaming each other's gang for the increased police activity surrounding their operations. Hemi had heard David Williams was moving up to Northland and was planning to run their northern operation. Even though Williams' death was supposedly an accidental overdose, Hemi knew differently. He knew there would be talk that members of the Northland Black Power may have done Williams in. Fucking Audrey! He knew if he didn't do something, there would be a gang war and it would be bad for his business. Hemi had a lot of power within the Kaikohe prison walls. He still had his contacts on the outside. When a member of a gang dies, their funeral is an event to behold. Hundreds of bikers from across the island congregated at the local Marae. David Williams was respected among his friends. His sudden death was the talk of the members of the Head Hunters. Many blamed rival gangs and the conflict over meth trade territories. The word was out Hemi Heke insisted the Black Power gang was not responsible and had sent his condolences to the Head Hunters. He also asked the members of Black Power to do him a favor. He knew they would oblige.

CHAPTER 80

Detective Inspector Bromley looked at the two men sitting opposite him. He was intrigued. "Important," they said, insisting they met at the station as soon as possible. By eight o'clock Bromley had already grabbed a quick bite to eat with his family and returned to his office.

He recognized Paul immediately as Poppy and Audrey's friend who had joined them at the restaurant. The other man, he learned, was Poppy's Uncle Barney who came prepared to the meeting with a folder full of papers.

The men sat in silence as Bromley opened the folder and methodically read each page. They had provided comprehensive notes, statements from inmates, lists of dates, times and places of the crimes Bromley was only too familiar with. Crimes he had solved. Crimes that had changed his life - promoting him to the position of Inspector, the position that gave him the recognition he enjoyed today. Crimes he had no desire whatsoever to reopen. Why? Why now? He had hoped Poppy's obsession would simply give way to acceptance. Instead she and her uncle had been digging into each case with vengeance resulting in what looked like enough proof to reopen at least four of the cases and put Audrey Wetherby on the suspect list.

As he turned over the last page, Barney handed him a memory stick, which he inserted into his desktop computer. He watched as timed photos taken from Sutton's front door documented the comings and goings of every person from before Williams' death to after his body was removed from the premises.

"Audrey Wetherby was there," said Barney. "This proves it."

"She has some serious explaining to do."

"What now?" Paul asked.

"First, I need time to review all these documents with my superiors. We will need to run our own investigation and confirm the information you have provided. If, these allegations are, in fact, true then we have a serial killer on our hands." *We also have people doing time for some of these murders. It will be messy. People lose faith in the police when we lock up the wrong guys. I am fucked!*

"Will you bring her in for questioning?"

Bromley knew Poppy would be biting at the bit for Audrey's arrest.

"Not yet. I don't want to do anything to spook her until we have concrete evidence she is responsible for at least one of these deaths. In the meantime, I suggest you all keep your distance. I am curious, why didn't Poppy come with you?"

"She wanted to but we thought she would try and influence you and we wanted your unbiased opinion of the material we have uncovered. I had promised to research the cases for her book and when she read the results and viewed the photos, she wanted to confront Audrey and get her to confess. I finally convinced her to let the police handle it. She wasn't happy. I think she blames the police for mishandling her brother's death. The only one she seems to have faith in, is you detective. I hope she isn't sorry. This woman needs to be put in jail. She is dangerous.

When the men left to join Poppy at the local pub, Bromley sat staring at papers on his desk. If what he was looking at was indeed factual, he had let a serial killer go rampart in his town. It wasn't just his precinct that would be held responsible but all the precincts in the far north. He looked at the sheer number of crimes. *We fucked up, big time!* Bromley realized his life as he knew it would be changed forever. If only he had taken Poppy's accusations more seriously, maybe he could have put a stop to it before it got out of hand. Now too many people were involved.

The detective closed the file, turned out the lights and returned to the sanctuary of his home next door. It wouldn't be long before his family and the whole country knew he had let them down. He shuddered knowing the woman he had confided in, -had been almost friends with, and who had been only too willing to assist him with his inquiries over the years, was laughing at him behind his back. *Well Audrey Wetherby your days are numbered.*

CHAPTER 81

Counting her lucky stars, Audrey lay on the floor with a bottle of champagne and stared at the ceiling. She realized it was becoming a habit but it felt comforting somehow. Knowing she had taken control and eliminated people who had done her wrong, or who had simply pissed her off, felt remarkably satisfying. When Paul called to cancel, she was secretly pleased. Entertaining was exhausting. She could only play social Audrey in small doses. Tonight she needed her murder map. The projector light flickered on the ceiling creating a bluish white gleam in the darkened room.

Ever since she saw Poppy searching in the doorway next door she had an ominous feeling of doom. It became accentuated when Paul phoned to cancel dinner this evening. Silly really. If Poppy knew anything Audrey knew she would be the first one to confront her. Or would she? Audrey hadn't killed her damn brother. She hadn't even seen him the night he died. But what did that matter? Poppy just didn't want to leave it alone. *What was she searching for? Paul said something has come up. What? Did they know something?*

Audrey turned off her computer, turned on the lights and called Mei. "Mei, what are you up to? Want some company? Great! I'll be right over." She needed to shake off her black mood. She liked Mei. She could also check out the doorway entrance and see if she could spot what Poppy was looking for.

Nothing. There was nothing at the doorway. Mei was pleased to see her. "I am going crazy here. I don't know what to do all day. I downloaded a road code off the web and will sit my drivers' license soon. At least I will be able to take the car and go places."

"We need to find you an interest. I have an idea." The two women sat and drank wine and Mei talked about her life in China and how she missed her parents and her friends.

"I can't wait to bring my family over here," she said excitedly.

"Is everything going OK with the estate?" Audrey asked.

"Yes. Guy has been so helpful. Tomorrow he is bringing over the bank papers for my signature and I will be access Steve's accounts."

"I am so pleased for you Mei.

It was midnight before Audrey shone her torch down the grassy track back to Tiromoana. She had made a decision tonight. A decision that would change lives.

CHAPTER 82

Poppy sat at her computer in the window looking across at Doubtless Bay and marveled at the stillness of the harbor waters. How could such stillness exist when her whole being was in such turmoil? Ever since the guys returned from their meeting with Jimmy, she couldn't think straight. She had been the one to expose Audrey. It had been her determination and tenacity that uncovered the evidence that would put her away for life. She had dared to question the authorities, dared to stay at Tiromoana where Audrey had murdered her guests. Dared to walk her beaches where Audrey had dumped bodies. Just the mere fact that she was alive and writing her book was a miracle.

Poppy was meeting Paul and Uncle Barney for breakfast at the corner restaurant. She was becoming fond of Mangonui. Such a quaint, friendly village. She had visited the Art Center on the main road and was in awe of the local artists' work. The hundred-year-old Community Library was housed in one of the Heritage buildings along the waterfront. She had even taken the

Heritage trail through bush tracks and past the old school house and up the Maori Pa overlooking the bay.

The views were breathtaking. It was difficult to understand that in this peaceful paradise so many murders had taken place.

The men were waiting at their usual table. They stood when she approached the table. "We ordered you coffee and a breakfast bagel," her uncle said.

"Thanks." Poppy took the seat facing the bay appreciating the men who kept the best seat for her. "So when do you think Jimmy will have all our evidence verified?"

"He said it would take a couple of days. He reminded us we should keep our distance in the meantime. I said I would call Audrey today. I'm not sure if I should see her, under the circumstances." Paul started on his second cup of coffee.

"We don't want her to suspect anything. She obviously knew we set up the cameras at Tiromoana. She knows I am on to her." Poppy nibbled at her bagel and returned it to the plate. "I can't eat. I am so worried she is going to get away with it again. What if the police decide it isn't enough?"

"I'll call her after breakfast."

"Be careful." Barney warned. "She is not stupid. She's been getting away with murder for years. You don't want to be her next victim."

CHAPTER 83

Superintendent Burt was pacing up and down the conference room. "Who is this guy? This Barney fellow?"

"He's a private investigator from Auckland. Has an excellent reputation. It was his niece, Poppy Perkins, who hired him. She is writing a true crime book about her brother, Eric Chapman's, murder. She has been researching the case for some time and her uncle agreed to help her. It was he who uncovered this information. He has a friend who works at the Kaikoe Prison. Barney Dugger's been interviewing inmates and close associates of the victims. Dugger has also done some work for the police in the past."

"Well it's a fucking embarrassment for the police." The Super glared at his colleagues. "What bloody fools we look like. I thought you all had this buttoned up." He looked at Detective Constable Driver and Detective Inspector Bromley. "You two! You are responsible for this major fuck up! The press is going to be all over this! A fucking woman who you both interviewed on numerous occasions, a fucking woman who should have been the main person of interest in all these cases. What were you fucking thinking? Morons! All of you! Fucking Morons!"

The two detectives knew they would be the ones to take the blame.

"So where do we go from here?" a voice asked from the back of the room.

"What we should have done in the first place. We are going to go through every piece of this evidence. Talk to everyone who has given a written statement here. Verify everything. Bromley, where is the woman now?"

"She is at her home in Hihi, I presume."

"You presume! You presume! You don't know! Put someone on her every minute of the day. We don't want her to disappear on us now."

"Will do." Bromley realized he was still in denial that Audrey was really guilty of all these crimes.

"Now!" the Super yelled. "Do it now!"

Bromley left the room and walked outside into the fresh air. He called his station and put a team on twenty-four-hour surveillance of Audrey. "You will need someone at the entranceway and at all beach accesses. Keep out of sight. No cars parked on Peninsula Road. The area is completely isolated and any police presence will be as obvious as a beached whale."

The meeting finally dispersed. Bromley and Driver left with their reputation in ruins. "We should have seen it,' Driver said. "She was involved in every case. I talked to her on so many occasions. I even suspected her at one time but she had an answer for everything, an alibi every time and that damn pleasant way she has to convince you she is Ms. Helpful. Fuck! She's good."

"At least you only have two murders in your district in question. I have too many to count. We know about these ones. What about all the murders we don't know about?"

"Don't even go there."

CHAPTER 84

Paul dialed the number and waited. No answer. He left a message; "Audrey, sorry about last night. Thought you might like to join me for lunch in Russell. We could take the boat over from Pahia and eat at the pub over there. Get back to me. It is almost ten. I could pick you up at noon. Hope you get this message." *Damn, I rambled on.*

At eleven she called; "Sorry Paul. I just picked up your message. I would love to take the ferry to Russell. Great! See you at noon."

She appeared in a daisy floral dress, yellow floppy hat and high-heeled sandals. She looked beautiful. He opened the door for her and she slid onto the passenger seat, removed her hat and let her soft blonde hair fall loose almost to her shoulders. Her skin was tanned from days of sun. She smiled as she leaned over to open his door for him. She looked happy. Happy and relaxed.

The hour drive to Pahia was remarkably enjoyable considering Paul had trepidations about spending the afternoon with a beautiful serial killer.

Yesterday Detective Inspector Bromley had asked for his help.

Knowing he had been spending time with Audrey on a personal basis he suggested Paul take Audrey out for the afternoon while his team search Tiromoana. What they were looking for Paul could only imagine. Maybe collect Audrey's DNA, check for any sign of previous trauma. He doubted Audrey would be stupid enough to leave any evidence in her house but he had agreed to help.

The ferry pulled alongside the old wooden dock at Russell. Paul and Audrey disembarked along with a string of tourists enjoying the sights of the Bay of Islands.

Russell was the original capital city of New Zealand steeped in Maori and early European history. The Duke of Marlborough Hotel was formally an unlicensed 'grog shop' owned by an ex-convict in 1827. Paul thought it an appropriate last lunch venue for them. The detective said they should have enough evidence to arrest Audrey as soon as tomorrow. They ordered the Dukes Seafood Chowder and salad complimented with a cold glass of Sauvignon Blanc.

Audrey touched their glasses and toasted to good friends. Paul felt guilty "To good friends," he repeated.

CHAPTER 85

udrey's cottage was unlocked when the police arrived shortly after noon. They had waited until they spotted Paul's car driving up Hihi Road before they made their way to the secluded property. The cars were unmarked and their presence was kept to a minimum. They had specific instructions as to what they were looking for. Her DNA could be collected from the hairbrush in her bathroom. There were multiple toothbrushes in a cup in the bathroom. They removed one. They checked her computer expecting it to be as benign as it was. Nothing! Just business paraphernalia; reservations, marketing and guest lists. Safari and Google Chrome had no history. She had obviously deleted her searches. Why?

They shone Luminal – a black light in the cottage and were suddenly standing under a ceiling of glowing stars. "Fucking Milky Way in here! What's it with all the bloody stars?" They laughed.

Finding nothing, no traces of blood or any evidence linking Audrey to any of the crimes they left with their DNA samples and headed back to the station ensuring they left the cottage exactly as they found it. Detective Inspector Bromley sent off the samples for DNA analysis. He had sent off anything and everything he could find from each of the cases in question for additional DNA testing. If Audrey's DNA matched any of the samples taken from the crime scenes they would have what they needed to take her into custody. They should have the results in sixty hours. He couldn't afford to mess up now. Paul Riley's help was paramount. He was due back with Audrey about now. He checked his phone. It was five o'clock.

The last twenty-four hours had been hectic. A special task force was set up in Whangarei. Every case where Audrey Wetherby was part of the investigation was reopened and scrutinized. The list was depressingly long. Bromley blamed himself. He was responsible for many of the cases for which he had arrested innocent people and they were serving time. He knew his job was on the line.

CHAPTER 86

Audrey returned home feeling exhilarated and just a little tipsy. Paul had insisted they share another bottle of wine and she knew she had drunk more than her fair share. He had explained why he had cancelled their dinner. It was Poppy. She and her uncle were leaving – returning back to Auckland today. It was a farewell dinner. Paul said he wanted to see Audrey before he left. He was due to leave tomorrow morning.

"So Poppy has left?" Audrey was pleasantly surprised.

"Yep. She has been offered a job at the Auckland Herald."

"Good for her. And you? Are you back to work tomorrow?"

"No. I am in between careers. I thought I might take a trip overseas for a while. See the world."

"Sounds divine."

"And you, Audrey? What are your plans? Have your repairs been completed? Is it back to business?"

"Yes, back to business. Are you staying the night?"

Paul looked ill at ease, trapped "I have a few things I have to do before I leave tomorrow" he was obviously lying.

"At least stay for one more drink" Audrey insisted.

"Just one and then I must be going."

Audrey left Paul sitting at the picnic table on the front lawn. The bay was still and calm creating an atmosphere of tranquility.

Audrey sensed danger. She could smell it. Paul had changed. He hadn't touched her all day. Oh, he smiled and joked and talked affectionately, but his body language was a dead giveaway. She expected him to stay the night. He seemed almost afraid of her. What was going on? She reached for the tin marked "sugar" and removed a small sachet almost identical to the rest. The white powder dissolved into his wine. She needed time to think.

She called Paul inside. "I need to eat something. Just a snack. Come on in."

Paul lay on her chaise chair and listened to Leonard Cohen's "You're My Man" as Audrey prepared a cheese and fruit platter. She gave him one more chance to show her physical affection. Sitting on the edge of the chaise chair she leaned over to kiss him. He turned his head and sipped his wine. *He knows!*

Half an hour later, Paul was fast asleep and she was looking through his phone. She scanned through his messages. *They know, they all know.* She looked up at the ceiling.

CHAPTER 87

M ei and Guy were sitting on the deck watching the evening sunset. Mei realized she was happy. Audrey had been such a wonderful help with all the legal stuff even attending the meeting with her and Guy earlier in the day. Having Audrey as a friend had saved her sanity. She was there for her. She helped her see a future Mei hadn't even dreamed about. She had a lot to thank her for.

Guy had suggested after the estate was transferred to her, and his role in the process was over, maybe they could continue their relationship on a more personal basis. Mei said she needed some time to heal after all the trauma. She wanted to live independently – more like Audrey. Be her own boss. Answer to no-one. Be free. Guy understood and said he was a patient man.

As soon as Guy left, Mei decided to walk over to Audrey's. She saw Paul's car in the driveway and didn't want to disturb them. She knew Audrey liked Paul. Instead she returned to her house and ran a nice hot bath. Her wounds were healing and her strength was coming back.

Guy had managed to release Steve's bank information. She

was now a signee on all his accounts. Mei was shocked to find Steve had over two million dollars in liquid assets. Money was never going to be problem again.

Guy had taken her out for a driving lesson and offered to get her prepared for her test next week. She picked up her phone and called her parents. Mei couldn't wait to share her good news. This morning she had purchased their airline tickets. They would be arriving in Auckland in just a few days. She looked around her spacious house. They will love it here. They will be so proud of me. She knew it would be difficult to explain they were going to be grandparents, but she welcomed her child into her new world and knew they would too.

Chapter 88

Audrey needed just a little more time. She looked at Steve sleeping peacefully. What a shame he had turned out like all the other men in her life. Betrayal. She was familiar with it. They were all the same. She knew one thing. If Detective Inspector Bromley wanted her out of the house today, he would have searched her cottage and office. She smiled. *They must think I'm stupid.* They would find nothing. She never left a trace. The question now was what would she do with Paul? The detective knew he was with her. Were they watching her? What did they have on her? It can't be Poppy. Paul said Poppy was leaving today. It must have been the police who found the camera next door. Did they have photos of her entering and exiting the house on the day of Dave Williams' death? Was that what all this was about? But she had covered herself with the story she gave Mei. What were the police looking for?

She was tired. She knew Paul wouldn't wake until morning. He was leaving tomorrow. She knew she would never see him again.

Paul's phone beeped it was a text from Detective Sutton. "Paul, we are getting concerned. You haven't checked in."

Audrey sent him a text "All OK. Meet you at the Mangonui Inn." She looked at his room key. "Room 6 at 11p.m. Paul."

Paul would be asleep for hours. She put her hair up into a baseball cap and changed into his jacket. Leaving him on the chaise chair she picked up his keys and drove his car down the drive. Cops were everywhere. They were in plain clothes but so easy to spot. One at her gate pretending to be on a nightly stroll. He waved as she passed. Another cop down at the Hihi Motor Camp. Also gave her a nod. A plain cop car sat on the Hihi turnoff. They were obviously aware of Paul's car and let her head onto the main road towards Mangonui. When she reached the Mangonui turnoff she headed straight ahead. She knew she had at least two hours before they would be searching for her. She just had to make it to Kaitaia by ten.

She did a mental check that she had everything she needed. She did. She would stop at the small motel in the next town and change into her new identity. It was just on nine.

CHAPTER 89

Detective Sutton relaxed when he got Paul's text. He had begun to doubt his decision to suggest Paul spend the afternoon with Audrey. He notified the guys on duty that all was OK. They radioed back to say they had spotted Paul's car heading towards Mangonui. He breathed a sigh of relief. He had a couple of hours before meeting him at the Inn. Everything was going to plan. They had everything almost buttoned up for tomorrow. She was going nowhere tonight. He had all the streets around Hihi covered. There was only one way out onto the main road.

Her hair analysis was already in. It matched a hair taken from the car a few years ago at one of the crime scenes. There was also a match with a hair pulled from the clothes of another victim. It was enough to arrest her and take her in. They were not going to take any chances and had called in the armed defenders squad to assist with the arrest. Two of her victims had been shot. She could have a gun hidden anywhere on her property. He was not going to add to her victim count. It was going to be over by lunchtime tomorrow.

He radioed his team at Hihi "Better keep close to the cottage tonight. We don't want her to take off. Make sure you cover both beaches too. But keep your distance. We don't want to give her any indication we are on to her.

Thank goodness Hihi is so remote. The news media would have a field day if they knew Hihi was the host town of a local serial killer. He checked his phone. He wondered what Paul Riley had to say – why he wanted to meet him tonight. Must be important. He checked his phone. It was nine o'clock. He had time to pop home, grab a cup of coffee and check in with his wife. She had been complaining about his distant mood lately. When this was over, he needed to sort out his marital situation. He wondered if Poppy might like to take a trip away somewhere. The thought made him smile. Maybe after he met with Paul he would stop by and visit her. He texted her. "What are you doing after eleven? Feel like some company?"

She texted right back, "Nothing and yes."

At ten forty-five he got a text from Paul. "Pretty tired. Let's meet up tomorrow. Paul."

He texted Poppy "I'm on my way."

CHAPTER 90

The small motel on the corner of state highway 10 and state highway 1 in Awanui was set back off the street. She parked Paul's car around the back and out of sight and covered it a large tarpaulin. She had booked the room for a week and paid cash. It would give her time before the covered car would create suspicion. Once inside her room she pulled the curtains and laid her suitcase on the bed. In the bathroom she dyed her blonde hair a dark shade of chestnut brown and cut it into a pixie style – short and spiky. She looked in the mirror. She looked completely different. Audrey always wore red lipstick and black eyeliner. This new girl wore little makeup and much cooler clothes. She put on a pair of ripped jeans, flat army boots, white t-shirt and army jacket. She compared her mirror reflection with the photo in her new passport. For the photos she had used a wig to create her new identity. She ran her fingers through her new short haircut and felt wonderful! It was time. Time to move on. She opened her new wallet and checked its contents; USA drivers license, USA passport, USA social security card and even credit cards in her new identity. Audrey Wetherby was now Anna

Ward. She knew this day would come and was prepared. The clothes, hair dye, wallet, documents, cash were always kept in a suitcase stored in a storage unit near the motel. Now she was Anna and lived in Montecito, California. She had already rented a small guesthouse on a five-acre horse ranch. The owner was happy to have the extra cash and she had paid six month in advance.

It was time to leave for the small airstrip. A private car pulled up to the main entrance of the motel. She was waiting. They drove to the door of the private jet and Anna Ward climbed aboard. It was only a twenty-five-minute flight to Auckland airport. She was booked on the midnight flight to LAX. First class all the way. She had already texted Detective Inspector Bromley to reschedule Paul's meeting. She had left the phone in his car at the motel making sure she had removed the Sims card. She didn't want them tracing the phone until she was already settled into her new life. She had given Paul enough GHB to knock him out until at least mid morning.

Once aboard the flight to California, Anna Ward ordered a glass of French champagne and settled in for the twelve-hour flight.

"Miss Ward, can I get you another drink before we depart?"

She looked at the pretty flight attendant. "That would be wonderful."

CHAPTER 91

Detective Inspector Bromley couldn't wipe the smile off his face. Last night had changed his life. Sex with Poppy was like no sex he had ever had before. Sure, he had loved his wife when they were first married. But Poppy - she was something else. She made him feel like a man. He only had a couple of hours of sleep, but he felt wonderful. When he got home at five am his wife was still asleep. She knew he was working on a big case. By seven o'clock he was up again and ready to take on the world.

He had scheduled a meeting at the Mangonui station with the whole team. Every detail was mapped out. They would enter the premises at ten o'clock. The property had been under surveillance all night. Audrey had not left. Her car was still in the car park outside her office. The curtains of the cabin were still closed. It would appear she was still asleep. As the team prepared for the take down, a call came through from their colleagues on the Hihi turnoff. "Inspector, we have a situation here. About fifty bloody bikers are heading into the Hihi township. They appear to be on a mission."

"Tell the guys down at the Motor Camp to stop them. I don't want them heading up Peninsula Road."

"Too late," came from the other car "They are on their way up towards Tiromoana. Maybe they are going to Sutton's old property next door. We are following them."

"Fuck!" Bromley was outraged. "We don't need them screwing things up. Try and head them off."

"Easier said than done. The road is narrow and they are kicking up some serious dust. Must be about sixty bikers and they look like they mean trouble."

"I am sending you back up now." Bromley knew this wasn't good. He only had a couple of guys at the Tiromoana property. They were no match for a biker gang.

His officer at the Tiromoana entrance managed to close the gate just before the first biker reached it but as the bikers began to congregate at the entrance, he realized it was futile to try and stop them from entering the property. They forced open the gate and headed up the long driveway.

CHAPTER 92

M ei awoke to the first day of the rest of her new life.
She dressed in her best outfit and headed across to
Tiromoana. It was just on eight o'clock and the sun
was beginning to warm the early breeze.

She used her key to open the office. Looking around she felt a
sense of pride. This was all hers now. Audrey had shown her how
to use the reservations program and how to update the website.
She sat at the computer and checked the bookings. She had a full
day before the first guests arrived. The holiday season would soon
be upon her. The cabins were fully booked for most of the peak
season. Tomorrow four of the six cabins were booked. She
checked the phone for messages and headed next door to the
cottage. Audrey had shown her where she kept the key. Mostly
she never bothered to lock the cottage. "It's always safe here in
Hihi," she would say. "The neighbors keep an eye out for each
other." She knew that was true but now she owned the two
adjoining properties and the nearest neighbor was at least two
miles away.

Audrey had left the curtains closed. Mei opened them and let the sun shine in. She opened the sliding door to the master bedroom and saw him asleep on the chaise chair.

"Paul. Wake up," she shook his arm. "Paul. Why are you here?"

He didn't move. He seemed to be in a deep sleep. She tried several times and began to get concerned. Why won't he wake up? "Paul." It was no use. She decided to just let him sleep and set about making them both a cup of coffee.

While the coffee brewed she took a walk around the cabins. Opening each door, she aired the rooms and checked for anything that required servicing. Audrey had left them ready for the next guests complete with wine in the fridge and welcome notes on their coffee tables. She was such a professional. Mei hoped she could run the business as well as her.

Mei was flattered when Audrey said she would like to sell the business to her. Mei wanted something to do. Something she could feel proud of. Owning Tiromoana Cabin Resort gave her a purpose. Also owning a business and the large property next door would hasten her permanent residency Guy had told her. She was also carrying a New Zealand baby.

Mei had plans. She would extend the business by adding cottages to the property next door. She had already sketched out designs for a swimming pool and spa. Massages, manicures, hair-dressing and a full health spa would entice elite travelers. More importantly, she had a purpose, something of her own.

Returning to the cottage, Mei attempted to wake Paul. She was beginning to be concerned. After an hour she decided to call for help. She called the nearest doctor's office and they suggested she call 111 for an ambulance. Mei drank her coffee and sat beside Paul and waited.

The stillness of the morning was shattered by the roar of

motorbikes and wail of sirens. Mei heard the deafening growl of motors getting closer and closer as they thundered up Peninsula Road. It was frightening. She shook Paul. "Paul, Paul, wake up. Please wake up!" she needed him. Then she knew they were coming up the driveway. She looked out the window and realized she was in deep trouble. Were they friends of David Williams? How did they find out she was at Tiromoana? Were they here to hurt her? She watched as the men stepped off their bikes and congregated around her office. They wore patches. She wasn't familiar with their gang. But they looked like they were there to make trouble. She took a deep breath and went to answer the door.

The man was huge, bald, tattooed and angry. "We're looking for Audrey." He told her.

"Audrey does not live here anymore. I am the new owner. Can I help you?"

"Since when? When did you become the new owner?" The man looked pissed.

"Since today. Today is my first day. Why are you looking for Audrey?" she dared to ask.

"I don't believe you." The man pushed passed Mei and walked inside the cottage. He saw Paul still asleep on the chaise chair. He kicked him "Fucking get up." He said kicking him again. "What's his problem?" he asked Mei.

"I don't know. I found him here when I arrived this morning. He won't wake up. I called an ambulance I think it is arriving now." She turned to see the ambulance pulling up in the driveway.

"Where is Audrey?" the man asked as he walked from room to room. "Where has the bitch gone?"

"I really don't know. She didn't tell me."

The man looked at her more intently. "Hey you're not the

Chink girl who fucked over Williams and got his old man's property?

Mei was shocked. If this was David Williams' gang she was in trouble. "You must have me confused with someone else."

"We are just here to set things right. That bitch Audrey is the reason our mate is in jail. She set him up.

The ambulance guys came to the front door and she ushered them in. The sheer commotion had caused the police to arrive also. Tiromoana was buzzing with police, medics and bikers. It was chaos. Mei ushered the medics to where Paul lay sleeping oblivious to his surroundings.

"Has he been drinking? Taken any drugs?" they asked.

"I found him here when I arrived this morning,"

she explained. "I have just purchased this business. This is my first day. His name is Paul Riley. He was a friend of the previous owner. She no longer lives here. I was worried when I couldn't wake him so I called you."

The medics put him on a stretcher and carried him out to the ambulance. Bikers were now sprawled out on the front lawn. They looked as though they were there to stay a while.

As the ambulance drove slowly down the driveway, Detective Inspector Bromley appeared in her doorway. "Mei what are you doing here?"

"I am so pleased to see you. I don't know what to do. All these bikers have just arrived. Can you get them to leave? They are looking for Audrey, but I explained to them that I am the new owner of Tiromoana. Audrey no longer lives here."

She watched the detective's face turn ashen. "Audrey is not here?"

"No, I have been trying to explain to everyone. I am the new owner. Audrey no longer lives here. She sold the business to me. I have no idea where she has gone."

"When was the last time you saw her?

"Yesterday morning. She signed over the business to me. My lawyer, Guy Morris, had already drawn up the sale and purchase agreement. I took possession just a couple of hours ago."

"I saw an ambulance leaving. What was that about?"

"When I arrived this morning, I found Paul Riley fast asleep on a chair in the cottage. I couldn't wake him. He had passed out completely. I called an ambulance. They are taking him to the Kaitaia hospital they said."

"Paul Riley was here?"

"Can you please ask the bikers to leave? They scare me. I need to tidy up before the guests arrive tomorrow. They are making a mess of the lawns with their bikes. Please," she begged.

It took two hours before the police checked every cabin and every inch of the fourteen acres before they were satisfied Audrey Wetherby was not on the property. They also got permission from Mei to check her property next door. By late afternoon the police had left Hihi and were on their way back to Mangonui. The bikers followed figuring they were on a wild goose chase. If the cops couldn't find her there was no chance they would.

Mei realized her heart hadn't stop racing since she found Paul asleep on the chair at eight that morning. Her first day had been a nightmare. Why was everyone looking for Audrey? The detective wouldn't tell her. The biker had said Audrey was responsible for their friend being in jail. She decided to call Guy. Maybe having a man in her life would be easier here in New Zealand. It was a crazy place.

CHAPTER 93

Detective Inspector Bromley's team called every train station, bus station, airport and cruise liner. There was no sign of Audrey. He had put out her description nationwide. She had vanished. Paul had fallen into a coma. His doctor said there was no telling when he would wake up. Apparently, he had a reaction to the drug he was given. Bromley would have to wait to hear what happened back at Audrey's cottage the night she went missing. He was no fool he realized it had been Audrey who had driven Paul's car out of Hihi last night. She had driven right past all the guys on surveillance. She made them look like fools. They had yet to find Paul's car. It was a mess.

Superintendent Burt was on the warpath. He took over the case and set up a national task force. They contacted the FBI and put out an alert for the woman along with full description, DNA and recent photos. It would only be a matter of time.

By ten that night Bromley needed a break. He called Poppy. "Can I come by and see you?"

"Of course. I can't believe it. I heard it on the news. She has gone. Oh my gosh. Jimmy, what are you going to do?"

"I am going to find her. I am going to bloody find her."

"You will Jimmy. If anyone can, you can."

Poppy had been his saving light. Without her, Bromley's life would have simply fallen apart. He loved her. He loved her more than life itself. Maybe they could both go somewhere. Somewhere away from Mangonui, away from New Zealand. He had a cousin in Montana. *When this shit is over I'm out of here.*

She opened the door looking beautiful. "Jimmy, come in. I'm so sorry. It must be awful. I am so worried about Paul. Uncle Barney is at the hospital now. He thinks it is all his fault."

"If it is anyone's fault, it is mine. I was the one who suggested he spend the afternoon with Audrey while we searched her cottage. All the time she was planning her escape. You were right, Poppy. You were right all along."

"What is going to happen to Tiromoana. Did she just leave it?"

"She sold it to Mei. She was there when we got there this morning. Mei said Audrey signed the papers yesterday. I wonder how she knew we were on to her?"

Poppy looked sheepish. "It was I."

"What do you mean, it was you?"

"I put up spy cameras that looked like smoke alarms in her cottage and in our cabins. I thought I could find out what she was up to. But she found the cameras. She didn't say anything. She just took them down and replaced them with new fire alarms. I'm sure she checked the memory cards. She would have known I was on to her. Who knows what she found out about me. My book. I guess she also knew Paul was on to her too. Poor Paul." Poppy looked terrible.

Jimmy put his arms around her. "Poppy, you know you mean the world to me."

"Thanks, Jimmy". She snuggled into his chest. "The only good thing about all of this is that I have met you."

"After this is over, we need to talk – about us."

"You must find her, Jimmy. She needs to be locked up for life. Only then can my brother rest in peace."

EPILOGUE

Time has a way of healing. The news Audrey Wetherby was a suspected serial killer, who allegedly was responsible for multiple murders in the Northland area, was front-page news for months. Her two sisters in New Zealand wouldn't comment and her sister in London was adamant she couldn't hurt a flea.

"Rubbish. It's all rubbish. Audrey is a kind and loving person. Ask anyone who knows her," the pretty brunette interviewed by BBC said. "And no, I haven't seen her or heard from her in over a year."

DNA from a number of crime scenes were linked to Audrey and the suspected perpetrators who had already been tried and convicted for the crimes were set free.

Detective Inspector Bromley, the lead investigator in a number of the cases linked to Audrey Wetherby, retired and moved to America with his new wife, Poppy Perkins. They say the detective never recovered from the guilt of convicting innocent people for Ms. Wetherby's numerous crimes.

Poppy Perkins, now Poppy Bromley, released her best seller,

"The Audrey Murders" becoming a popular true crime author and regular panelist on numerous crime television shows.

Paul Riley recovered from his ordeal and joined his friend, Barney's, private investigator's firm. Their reputation of handling the Audrey murder investigation brought them instant notoriety and continued financial success. Most weekends they can be seen cruising out in the Northland waters.

Mei Wong opened the new Tiromoana Resort and Spa with phenomenal success. The one-hundred-acre resort became New Zealand's most popular international tourist accommodation venue in the far north. Private chalets, swimming pool, spa, restaurant, boat trips, secluded beaches and regular murder mystery dinners featuring the infamous Audrey Wetherby continues to be a popular event.

Sightings of Audrey Wetherby still continue to be reported. But to date, New Zealand's most infamous serial killer has yet to be brought to justice.

THE END

ALSO BY LEONIE MATEER

THE AUDREY MURDERS – BOOK SERIES

The Murder Suite —Book One

The Cabin by the Sea — Book Two

The Murder Trail — Book Three

Murder in the Family — Book Four

The Murder Trap — Book Five

Murder in Lockdown — Book Six

The Taupo Bay Killings — Book Seven

If you enjoyed this book, I would be so appreciative if you would write a brief review on Amazon. Thank you.

Leonie Mateer

www.leoniemateer.com

About the Author

Puppeteer, children's entertainer, model agency owner, TV talk show panelist, luxury accommodation owner, entrepreneur, product developer, brand developer, storyteller, author, and indie publisher Leonie Mateer has lived a full and diverse life.

Born and raised in New Zealand, Mateer moved to the United States in her thirties to pursue business opportunities. She returned to New Zealand for several years in the 2000s, running a luxury lodge in Northland—which has been an inspiration for her crime series—and now splits her time between Northland, New Zealand, and the United States.

Mateer is known for her huge success as a brand development expert. She received 'Who's Who' awards from both Leading American Executives and American Inventors in the 1990s. As the creator of the brand Caboodles™, a teen girl brand that took the retail industry by storm in the late 1980s and early 1990s, she created a new retail category—the cosmetics organizer category —with Caboodles' global retail sales exceeding US$100 million worldwide.

Ms. Mateer also works in the real estate industry, specializing in residential and lifestyle properties in New Zealand's winterless far north.

Her two daughters and four grandsons live in the United States and are a constant inspiration for many of her stories.

OTHER TITLES BY LEONIE MATEER:

Business:

The Caboodles Blueprint – Turn Your Idea into Millions

Have a Product Idea? – How Many Could You Sell? – a collection of business articles.

Health and wellbeing:

Psoriasis – The Simple Cure – Who Knew?

Psoriasis - Staying Clear - The Healthy Alternative – a must read for any psoriasis sufferer.

Fiction:

"The Audrey Murders" – a seven book series starring Audrey Wetherby, a serial killer living in idyllic small towns in New Zealand.

Children's fiction:

The Magical World of Dantonia

Black Lake

The Bird Boys

Mason's Secret

Tarot Card Online Game

www.readyourownfortune.com

A do-it-yourself game that enables players to read their own fortunes online, anytime, anywhere. Her sixty-three-card deck, based on ancient fortune telling cards, has been deciphered with the assistance of professional psychics.